OBSESSION

ADDICTION DUET BOOK TWO

VIVIAN WOOD

AUTHOR'S COPYRIGHT

Copyright Vivian Wood 2017

May not be replicated or reproduced in any manner without express and written permission from the author. This ebook is licensed for your personal enjoyment only. This ebook may not be re-sold or given away to other people. If you would like to share this book with another person, please purchase an additional copy for each recipient. If you're reading this book and did not purchase it, or it was not purchased for your use only, then please return to author and purchase your own copy. Thank you for respecting the hard work of this author.

OBSESSION

1

SEAN

Sean shifted on the hard metal bench. He rested his head in his hands and ignored the pinch that still lingered from the handcuffs. With a sigh, he raised his head and tugged at the uncomfortable tie that felt more like a noose.

Wearing a suit in a jail cell seemed like a joke. He'd never wondered how the inmates featured on television switched from street clothes to ill-fitting suits, but now he knew. Lawyers. They could make anything happen.

He'd been blackout drunk during the entire thing. Well, mostly. He remembered little glimpses of the arrest, sparks of light and recognition. But he couldn't trust himself or his head. How much of it had really happened?

The reports his lawyer had gone over with him hadn't mentioned her, but he knew she'd been there. Harper had appeared like a saving grace, but it had been too late. That had been two weeks ago, and the scent of shame still clung to him tightly.

He remembered being drunk, or getting there at least. It had been all shiny, fuzzy and warm, a safe cocoon that had felt like home. He vaguely remembered the police showing up, but not the finer details. Sean knew he should have felt some kind of fear when they'd appeared, but the whiskey had numbed it all.

It hadn't been until Harper showed up, that look of horror on her face, that he'd started to come out of the stupor. It had shot him clean through, straight to his heart. He'd tried to force out the right words, to apologize, but he couldn't be sure he'd managed to say anything at all. *And what does she think of you now?*

Two weeks. It had been two weeks, and every waking minute since then all he could think about was how sorry he was. When Connor showed up, it had been all business. Sean sure as hell didn't want to bring her up, and when Connor lightly broached the subject, Sean shut down. It was obvious Connor didn't want to be there, was embarrassed of his mess of a family and was simply going through the motions. *And who could blame him?* Their family was wholly fucked up. If one of them were to get out, of course it would be Connor.

He stood up when he heard the boots of the correction officer down the short hall. Even though the suit was his, it felt wrong. It had been expertly tailored, but something had happened in the past fortnight that made Sean feel like his body wasn't his. He felt like a phony.

"Harris, you're up," the officer said gruffly. Every time the bars of the cell opened with a loud groan, it sounded like a macabre announcement to the world.

His lawyer waited just outside the steel doors. She was one of the best in Los Angeles, but even though she was being paid a princely sum she always shifted restlessly like she was doing Sean a favor. Her name was something exotic, stuffed with sounds that were foreign in Sean's mouth. He thought of her as T, T for tidy in her little black suit, and just didn't call her by name aloud.

"Mr. Harris," she said stiffly, "this way." As they walked toward her car, another compact little machine just like her, she rehashed the charges. "… assaulting an officer and being under the influence …"

Well, he knew that was right. He *had* punched that cop, but it had been right after Ashton had tried to blame him for the drugs. *What the hell had they expected him to do?*

"… *and* the original crime of being under the influence, and possession with intent to distribute …"

He opened his mouth to argue, but clamped it shut again. That charge was bullshit. It had been almost an ounce of cocaine, that was it. Ashton could have shoved that up his nose in a week, easy. And the prescription Adderall with some random girl's name on the bottle? He'd never figured out where the hell that had come from. The handful of Valium was a mystery, too. It had to have been some of Ashton's stash, because Sean never touched that shit. *I'm just a drunk*, he wanted to yell. *Not a fucking pill and blow junkie.*

"… the charge with the theft of Adderall, and using a prescription that isn't yours, along with possession of a controlled substance …"

Would you just shut the fuck up? But Sean listened, dutifully, as T continued to tick off the charges. She was fed up with him, he could tell. And Sean had started to consider whether maybe the scripts really had been his. Or, more accurately, that he'd stolen them. He'd been so fucked up on fifths of whiskey every day back then, who knew what he'd done? Maybe he had stolen those pills, or even a prescription pad, but he didn't have a clue.

"So?" T asked impatiently as she maneuvered toward the courthouse. "Have you decided yet? Guilty, not guilty, no contest? This is unprecedented, you know, refusing to give me an answer—"

"I told you," he said as rage bubbled inside. "I'm innocent of anything having to do with drugs. But everything from the day of the arrest is my fault. The assault, being drunk, all that." He looked out the window as green parks whipped by. It might be the last time he'd see them.

He saw her purse her lips from the corner of his eye. T glanced at him and something in her face softened. "You're a first-time offender," she said softly. "You probably won't get much time. Unless you want to make trouble."

"I don't," Sean said quickly.

"Okay. Well, stay quiet unless the judge asks you a direct question." T parked the car in a reserved spot and slapped a small sign onto the dashboard. "The judge is friendly, so hopefully we'll get good news today. My goal is for less than half of the charges to stick."

Sean nodded as T led him toward the special entrance for arrested defendants.

He'd imagined a scene like in a movie, a courtroom with rich mahogany wood everywhere and a big, thick desk he'd sit behind with T. It wasn't like that. Instead, he was ushered into a room that was absolutely filled with people, T by his side. She directed him onto a bench where he was squeezed next to a large blonde woman who smelled of cheap perfume.

The judge, a burly man who looked like he doubled as Santa Claus in December, was already naming a punishment for a girl who looked like she couldn't be older than eighteen. She hung her head and let the greasy locks hide her face.

"Uh ..." he muttered and leaned toward T. She shushed him quickly.

As the bailiff called up the next defendant, this one a slim black man dressed in a suit that looked bespoke, Sean scanned the crowd. Some of them looked like criminals, and hadn't even bothered to dress up. Others looked like accountants, mothers, yoga instructors and teachers. *You never could tell.*

He spotted Connor and Sam, though Sam seemed enraptured by the judge. Connor gave him an awkward smile and nod. But there was no sign of Harper. He felt his shoulders sag at the realization. *Of course she didn't come. Why would she?* He hadn't done anything even close to what they'd accused him of, but he couldn't blame her.

"Sean Harris." The bailiff's deep voice boomed through the courtroom.

T grabbed his arm firmly. It felt like she had the strength to lift him up, even with her thin brown forearms and sky-high heels.

Sean listened to the click of those heels as he followed her to the front of the courtroom. He couldn't bring himself to look at Connor and Sam again, but he felt all eyes of the courtroom on him. Some were bored as they waited their turn, but others drank him in like they could really use some juicy gossip.

He'd only partially heard the charges of those who came before him. Compared to him, they were lightweights. There were traffic crimes, animal abuse charges, and simple DUIs that just involved alcohol. Sean wondered how many of these people were actually here for a crime, and how many wandered in for the drama. He hadn't realized that in most cases, these courtrooms were largely open. Just about anyone could sit in as long as they passed security at the door.

As the judge began reading the charges, he heard T's all-business voice. It was surprisingly soothing, but he couldn't concentrate on the words. *Just keep quiet, that's what she said to do.* That was easy enough.

Still, as he stood before the room with the chipped furniture and the probing eyes, all he could think of was Harper. He couldn't blame her. And wasn't that what he'd been afraid of all along? He'd get attached, she'd get attached, and then he'd fuck the whole thing up?

He should have listened to his gut. The whole mess was one self-fulfilling prophecy. He'd tried, he really had, for so long to push her away. He'd warned her, he'd showed her glimpses of who he really was—he couldn't have shown her the whole thing, that would have scarred her for life.

Behind him, somebody coughed and he heard the phlegm in their throat. Sean turned to see a downtrodden young woman, no older than twenty, with a glint of glee in her eyes. *What the hell are you so happy about?*

" ... not guilty to the charges of possession with intent to distribute ..." T's voice cut through his thoughts. Not guilty.

Who would believe that? It was true, but it was what everyone said.

Still, when he stole a look at the judge, he saw nothing. Just the broad face of a man who looked like he had heard it all.

How did it all get to this point?

2

HARPER

Harper watched the last of the cigarette crumble to dust between her fingers. P would never miss the ones she kept filching. Besides, he'd seemed to intuit for the first time in their long friendship her need for quiet.

P had been a sweetheart about the whole thing, she had to give him that. Unlike her catty roommates—all except Molly—he hadn't pushed and prodded when he'd heard about her life falling apart. His eyes hadn't lit up with the promise of some irresistible gossip. Instead, he'd quietly but firmly demanded that she move right in.

It was selfless, graceful, but that didn't make sleeping on the living room couch any more comfortable. Still, when your boyfriend just got arrested in front of you, any couch made a perfectly good place to plop down and cry.

That had lasted three full days, while Harper took breaks to lick at her wounds in the empty loft. P spent most of his days either at work in the leather shop or tucked away into one of the shared spaces he leased for designing.

Alone and all cried out, day four had turned into the day of perpetual cleaning. Harper looked around. It was like the past few days of nonstop cleaning had been pointless. *For my bestie, you really have some nasty guy habits,* she thought. P hadn't even said anything in the past week when he dragged himself home. The sudden lack of empty sugar-free energy drinks and used coffee mugs hadn't made an impression on him.

On the other hand, he was certainly doing his part on keeping pace with her. More nights than not, he came home drunk. Harper would stick her head under the thin blanket until she could figure out if he was alone or not. Whether P had company or not, it didn't stop him from rampaging through his loft while he dropped takeout gyros on the floor and fumbled for what he called a "gentleman's nightcap." On his worst nights, she spent most of the next day picking up his mess.

It was ten in the morning on a Tuesday when Harper flopped onto the couch after her morning cleaning session. The vibration of the Dyson vacuum still growled in her palms. She was exhausted, but if she scoured the want ads, at least she'd feel somewhat productive.

"Jesus, what the hell was that?" P emerged from his bedroom, gauzy violet bathrobe with lace-trimmed sleeves clinging tightly to his forearms.

"Oh my god!" Harper jumped into a seated position on the couch and instinctively tried to neaten up her sweats to look semipresentable. "I thought you were at work!"

"Bitch, since when do I work on Tuesday mornings? It sounded like there was a construction crew in here. But I don't see any hard hats. Besides, well, the morning wood—"

Harper threw a pillow at him while he made a display of his crotch beneath the silk folds. "It was your vacuum," she said.

"Huh. I didn't know I had one of those. God, can you get me some water? I'm hungover as hell."

She rolled her eyes and pushed herself toward the kitchen. The coolness of the concrete countertops brushed against the sliver of bare skin between her rolled-up sweats and tank top.

P had already draped himself over the couch when she returned with two bottled waters. "Want ads, huh?" he asked before he tossed the paper onto the coffee table. "How did the interview with Sophia go?"

Harper scrunched up her face. *How did it go? Sophia took one look at me and instantly started in about her expertise in anorexia.* Sure, she'd been nice about it. But within two minutes she'd said Harper wouldn't be "suitable for the job" until the situation was "resolved." She sighed. "It's not a good fit right now," she told P.

"Bitch. Her loss," he said as he downed the bottle in one chug. "So, uh … don't take this as a hint or anything, okay? But I'm assuming this means you also can't move. Especially with everything up in the air with Sean."

She groaned. The last thing she wanted to think about was Sean. "As far as I know, he's in jail," she said.

"You haven't talked to him?"

"No. Haven't heard from him at all." That was true. But she'd spent many sleepless nights thinking about the arrest.

"Good for you. Curiosity killed the cat. Luckily for me, I

don't have a pussy. Don't want anything to do with them. That's why I looked him up—"

"P!"

"What?" he reached for his notebook. "Don't act like you don't want to see." P went to a bookmarked page of recently released mugshots from LA County. And there he was—along with a long list of charges.

Harper was taken aback, even as P pushed the notebook into her hands. "This … this isn't right," she said. The list of charges was substantial, and most had nothing to do with that night. She focused her eyes away from his face, so striking even with the veil of alcohol over it. The raven in the flowers that creeped up his neck shot a pang of regret through her. "These charges …"

"Intense, right?" P said. He pushed himself up with a groan. "I have to get ready for the afternoon shift," he said. "But, babe?" P paused in the doorway to the small hallway. "You can stay here forever. You know that right? But you gotta figure out what you're gonna do with yourself."

"I know." She smiled up at P. "Thanks."

When P left, low-carb, no-sugar protein bars in hand, she went right back to the want ads. *P was right, get your shit together.* But there was nothing there for her. Everything required experience and degrees in industries she knew nothing about.

Harper had almost dozed off to a rerun of *Keeping Up with the Kardashians* when the bell blasted through the fog. She glanced at the video display on P's notebook, which lit up instantly with the ring. "Holy shit," she whispered. It was

Connor. She'd only met him once, but he was so striking she'd never forget him.

He looked impatient, and Harper scrambled for a hair tie as she raced to the door. At least she didn't have to look like a total mess. "Connor?" she asked at the intercom to the door. "Come on up."

Harper caught a glimpse of herself in the hall mirror and moaned. She tried to smooth out the wrinkles of the white cami, but it was no use.

The sudden hard knock at the steel door brought her back to reality. "Hi," she said shyly. "Come on in."

"Nice place," Connor said as he surveyed the loft. "Kind of messy, though."

"Yeah, my, uh … my roommate isn't much of a neat freak."

"So … how are you?" Connor asked. He sat awkwardly, perched on the edge of the couch.

"I'm fine … how did you find me?"

"I have to admit, you weren't easy to track down," he said. "The last address I could find for you was where all those models are staying. And some weird Russian lady."

"Yugoslavian," she corrected. *Stupid. Who cares?*

"Oh. Okay," Connor said. "Well, anyway, nobody there knew where I could find you. Or at least they wouldn't say. That Yugoslavian woman seemed really protective."

Harper smiled grimly at the mention of Helena. "Yet, here you are."

"Yeah," Connor said. "Sean was no help. He didn't want me to find you, didn't want to bother you. But ... I think you should know."

"Know what?"

"That he's being charged with a bunch of stuff he didn't do."

"I'm aware of that," Harper said coldly. Connor didn't need to know that she'd just been made aware that morning.

"Oh. Well ... Sean's attorney thinks that he could get off if he can show that he was going somewhere stable. In life, I mean. And ... I think it would be better if he had someone to talk to, when and if we get him free."

Harper raised her brow. "And you thought of me? *I'm* what you think is stable in his life? Was?"

He bristled at the tense correction. "You're the only person other than his sponsor that he knows well enough to live with out here. Sam and I can move here, but ... I wanted to try this first."

"Connor," she said, "I don't—Jesus, I don't even have a place for myself to live! I'm sleeping on this couch."

He glanced down, suddenly aware that he'd been lounging on her bed.

"I mean, I'm just staying here temporarily."

"I'm sure we can finance it," Connor said with a shrug. "This sounds really bougie, but money isn't really an object. We'll take care of the funding, and you'll be his 'stable place to live' for awhile."

No. There's no way I'm letting you bankroll me. Harper had always felt somewhat like a whore during some modeling campaigns. But this? This was way too close. "Can I think about it?"

"Of course!" Connor said, eager at her almost-yes. "Just don't think about it too long, okay? Because we're back in court the day after tomorrow."

They both looked up as heavy footsteps appeared in the doorway. P's overpriced sunglasses were perched on his shiny obsidian head. He clutched a paper bag in his hand. "Harper?" he asked as his eyes shot back and forth between them. "Who's this? I thought you might want some lunch on my break..."

"P! This is Connor, Sean's brother. He ... tracked me down."

"Oh! Sean's brother. Yes, I can see the resemblance," P said. He turned up the charm and started to preen.

"Good to meet you," Connor said as he stood up.

"I have enough for everyone! I went to that new Whole Foods by my work—"

"Sounds good, but I'm actually just leaving."

"Oh, well if you're sure—"

Connor couldn't get out of there fast enough. As soon as the heavy doors clicked shut, P turned on Harper. "What the fuck was that about?"

"He wants me to live with Sean." The words sounded foreign in her mouth.

"He *what?*" P's mouth dropped open.

"Just for a little while! So he can say in court that he has a stable environment to return to."

"Sweetie, *you* don't have a stable environment to go to. And all of a sudden you're supposed to change your entire life to do some guy a favor? Someone you haven't heard a peep from since his arrest?"

"Yep." She looked up at him bluntly.

"Look, I'm not here to tell you what to do. But you know you'll always have a place here. Just you, though."

"Thanks," she said. Harper began to toe the sharp-cornered edge of the table. "Really," she said. "I mean it."

P retreated to his bedroom. She heard shuffling in the drawers. *There's no way I can stay here forever.* She mulled over the offer in her head. It was generous, that was for sure. Still, there was a sting that the first time anyone in Sean's family had contacted her, it was for a favor.

But the feeling of security she'd had in his arms was impossible to resist. She missed it with a physical pang she'd never felt before. There was nothing like it.

How do you even know you'd feel the same way about him now? She fell back onto the couch and cradled her head in her hands. *What am I supposed to do?*

3

SEAN

Sean craned his neck up as the jail cell was opened. "Harris, you're being released," the guard said brusquely. "Not you, Johnson," he warned the newbie who'd shared Sean's cell for the past twelve hours.

"Fucker," the new guy muttered under his breath.

Sean pulled himself up wearily. "Released?" he asked. "What happened? My lawyer didn't—"

"I'm just a guard, not a messenger," the middle-aged man said. He shifted his weight. "You coming? Or you prefer to sit a spell more?"

Sean followed the beast of a man out the doors where he was reprocessed. A pretty, petite officer instructed him to sign for his phone and wallet, the only two items that had been in his possession during the arrest. He was lucky he'd had those, though the phone was long dead.

In the reception area, T, Connor and Sam jumped on him. Sam hugged him tight, though he'd only met her a few times.

Connor gave him the same boyish, shit-eating grin he'd known since childhood.

"How'd you do it?" he asked. "I didn't even know—"

As Sam let him go, he saw Joon-ki and Harper over her shoulder. His sponsor looked sheepish, but all was forgotten as he drank Harper in. *Goddamn, does she look gorgeous.* Somehow more amazing than his memories or fantasies could capture.

"Hey," she said, almost shyly, to the floor. She tucked a lock of fiery hair behind her ear and shifted her hips. Even beneath the flowing black miniskirt and leather jacket with the arms pushed up, he could make out the familiar curves of her body. To him, she may as well have worn nothing at all.

"What … what are you doing here?" She wouldn't meet his gaze, and he couldn't blame her. *What are you doing here? That's what you came up with?*

"Why don't we go outside?" T asked, an attempt to soften the blow.

On the concrete steps of the jailhouse, he let Connor wrap an arm around his shoulder. Joon-ki approached with arms open. It felt partly awkward and a little comforting.

"So, let's give you the rundown," T said. Everyone was aware that Harper hadn't hugged him. He could feel it in their body language. Instead, she kept to the perimeter of the circle, wary and uncertain.

"You're out on bail," T told him. "Connor paid it."

"It's nothing," Connor said quickly before Sean could protest or make promises of repayment.

"But it's only while I hash out a plea deal with the DA," she said. "Honestly, that might take some time. He's fresh out of law school and a total prick. Sorry. Anyway, until then, you're on house arrest."

House arrest. That wasn't so bad. Sean thought of the ankle monitors he'd seen on television.

Connor cleared his throat. "Sean, you'll be living with Harper."

"Excuse me?" Sean gave Connor a death glare. *Was this some sort of fucked up joke?*

"It's a new apartment," Connor said brightly, like he was trying to sell it to him. "I took care of it, it's furnished and everything. It'll help Sam and me out, too. We can stay put until the baby comes, and then—"

"Hold up," Sean said. He closed his eyes and commanded Connor to shut up. "What ... why ..."

T interrupted. "It wasn't easy getting to this point," she said. "The judge wants to see that you're in a stable environment, that you have somewhere safe to live while on house arrest. It was either Harper or your brother, and given Sam's condition, it just didn't seem right to force this on them."

"This, uh ... this is going to be our last trip out here for awhile," Sam said. She rested her hand on her pregnant belly. "My doctor says I shouldn't fly anymore after this."

"We have three hours," T said, "and then the police will arrive at your new apartment to fit you with an ankle monitor. My understanding is that Harper has already moved in?" She gave Harper a curious look, and Harper nodded numbly at the ground. "And you'd better be there. You hear me?" T asked.

"Yeah. I hear you." T gave a tight-lipped smile to the rest of the group and traipsed down the last of the stairs toward her car.

"I'm sorry, but I think I need to lie down awhile," Sam said. Connor put his hand on the small of her back.

"We'll catch up with you before we leave tomorrow. Okay?" Connor asked. "Harper, you got this?"

Both Sean and Harper nodded obediently in Connor's direction.

"I should get going, too," Joon-ki said. "But I'll check in with you daily, alright? Get that phone charged. We'll get back on those daily AA meetings as soon as you're off house arrest, and we'll set up virtual meetings until then."

"Right." Even now, he was embarrassed for Harper to hear those two little letters associated with him. AA.

For what felt like a full minute, he was left alone with Harper on the steps. "We, uh, we should get going," she said.

"Harper—"

"Seriously?" she turned and finally looked him in the eye. "We don't have time for this. Don't make everything worse by being late to get your ankle bracelet put on."

"I'm really sorry." It was all he could manage. But surely she could fill in the blanks.

"I saw your face when you saw me," she said slowly. "I saw your surprise in there. I know you didn't choose to contact me. That was all Connor."

"If you would just let me apologize—"

"For what, exactly?" she asked. There was a steeliness in her eyes as she crossed her arms over her chest. "For not calling me? For being shitfaced the last time I saw you? Or were you more worried about the fact that you were being arrested? Maybe it's the long list of drug charges that you've accumulated? Which part, exactly, are you apologizing for?"

She had him there. He wanted to say *all of it*, and he wanted to defend himself, but there was nothing to say. She'd silenced him with a fire he'd only guessed she carried deep inside.

She stalked toward a new Tesla and slipped into the driver's seat without another word. *Is this from Connor?* But he didn't dare speak.

As she weaved through traffic, he saw the neighborhoods get nicer and nicer. Finally, a sign for Brentwood appeared. The luxury high-rise was part of the classic neighborhood's latest reincarnation. Harper pulled into the parking deck and got out.

"Coming?" she asked, the disdain palpable in her voice.

"Is my brother paying for all this?" he asked. "This ... this car, the apartment—"

She gave a mean laugh. "No. You are," she said. "Apparently, you're quite wealthy. Who would have guessed?"

She jammed the button for the elevator and he was slammed back into silence.

He thought he'd told her that. Kind of. *It's family money, not mine!* he wanted to scream at her. But how did he explain that to his girlfriend? Or ex-girlfriend, whatever they were now?

Harper led him into the sleek apartment kitted out in

midcentury modern furniture. The tufted gray sofa, steel and glass tables, and the concrete flooring was all right on trend. He knew exactly who'd been responsible for finding this place. It had Connor written all over it. Sean couldn't even imagine what Harper thought of the place. He pictured her dream home to be a little Victorian with rich moldings and intricate décor at every corner. Though they'd never talked about things like that, he realized. How much did he really know about her? Suddenly, he was desperate to know every little detail, from her first grade teacher's name to whether she'd ever roller skated. But those words were still buried in his throat.

She must think he was the biggest poser, slumming it in a crappy little apartment and needling away his days at a tattoo parlor when he had millions of dollars at his disposal. Millions of his father's dollars.

4

HARPER

She tried to act unimpressed with the penthouse, but it was still a shock every time she saw it. When Connor had first sent her the photos, she tried to brush it off as creative photography even as P squealed at the location. The first time she'd arrived with nothing but three suitcases stuffed with her meager belongings, it had taken her breath away.

"You like it?" Sam had asked.

"Uh, yeah," she had said. Who wouldn't?

Even now, as Sean trailed behind her and her anger simmered just below the surface, she caught her breath at the sight of the too-perfect penthouse. It was like something out of a magazine. Gorgeous, and she was all too aware she didn't belong.

Harper hadn't known what to expect when Sean emerged from the jail cell. Would he be excited to see her? Sheepish, but with that smirk that let her know everything would be okay? She hadn't known, but she certainly hadn't expected him to flat out ignore her. Sprinkle in the thorny heartache and their complete lack of trust, and it didn't take long for a hurricane to brew inside her.

Harper strode through the living room, aware of his eyes on her back. Even at her biggest runway show, she'd never embraced so much height or taken up so much room. She tossed the keys on the sofa console table where they made a neat tinkle in the handblown glass bowl.

Immediately, Harper retreated to what she secretly called her side of the apartment. Connor knew what he was doing, alright. A penthouse with two master en-suites, equal in size and luxury, with a stretch of semineutral ground parading as the living room, dining room and kitchen.

Harper didn't give a damn about the lack of bedding in Sean's bedroom. She didn't even peek when Connor dragged the big bag with a duvet, pillows and sheets into the other room. Instead, she'd quickly torn into her own bedding, gifted from Connor, of course, and set about making "her room" as personal and safe as possible.

She clicked the push-button lock behind her, waltzed into the posh bathroom, and turned on the tap. As she sank to the floor, the sobs came before she could even curl up on the warm tiles with the radiant heat.

You shouldn't have yelled at him about the money, she chastised herself. After all, there were a million other things she could be pissed about—was pissed about. Screaming about his wealth just made her look like she was mad because he'd cut off any potential for gold digging when they'd been happy together.

Happy together. That was a funny thought. She shook her head and the tears splattered across the gray floor. *Having money is hardly a crime,* she thought. *And he certainly hadn't owed her any transparency in that regard.*

She should have known, anyway. The fancy dinners, what had to be an unbelievable sum to enter the sex party, that night at the hotel—how had she thought he'd afforded it? Had she hoped he was so much of a bad boy that he was bankrolling that lifestyle on a stolen credit card? Laundered money, what?

Harper sighed. Hiding the money had just been the last straw. Her heart was already overburdened, and it wouldn't have taken much at all to push her over the edge. When her tears had gone dry, she pulled herself up from the floor and examined herself in the mirror. Her eyes were puffy and her lashes damp. Streaked down her cheeks were black rivulets of mascara that was supposed to be waterproof.

In the unfamiliar closet that smelled of a strange cleaning solution, she flipped through the few dresses, skirts and blouses that had made it from her earlier move-in. She pulled out a simple sleeveless black maxi dress.

"You can do this," she told her reflection in the angled free-standing mirror. She looked like she was in mourning, and perhaps she was. "You can't hide in here forever."

Just as she'd pumped herself up enough to face him, she heard the doorbell ring and the click of the front door opening. Male voices mumbled, unintelligible from her quarters.

Harper stepped out lightly, barefoot, onto the concrete flooring of the living room. Two brusque parole officers talked to Sean as he sat on the couch. One leaned menacingly over him while one hand rested leisurely on a pistol. The other was crouched down to fit the ankle monitor.

She noticed Sean had changed out of the clothes he'd been arrested in. His hair looked slightly damp, and she gulped at the idea of him in the shower. *Get yourself together.* Something about the wornout denim jeans and the tight-fitting white shirt made her heart start to flutter. The officer rose up to reveal a clunky, blinking contraption that rested on Sean's Converse high-tops.

Harper moved to the adjacent, matching loveseat and perched on the edge while the officers ticked off the rules. " … home except for parole meetings … go outside the building and the monitor will go off … alcohol or drugs in your system will alert the monitor, too …"

Jesus. It really was house arrest. For the first time, Harper realized that meant Sean would always be here. If she were to avoid him, she'd have to leave. Suddenly the idea of it being "her home, too" seemed like a joke.

"What about AA?" he asked quietly. He'd positioned himself to face as far away from her as possible without pissing off the cops.

"We spoke to your sponsor about that," the bigger cop said. "You can leave for meetings, as long as it's at one of these ten locations in your area." He handed Sean a slip of paper. "We know exactly when and where these meetings happen and how long they last. Given the radius, you have exactly twenty minutes from the official ending time to get back here. Understand?"

Sean nodded, like he'd been reprimanded by a schoolteacher.

"If you want to go anywhere else, it's on a case-by-case basis. And your PO, me, needs to be notified at least forty-eight hours in advance. Got it?"

"I got it," he said.

The officers never acknowledged her. She didn't know if that was a good thing or a bad omen. She watched their backs retreat toward the fancy entryway. It felt odd, to be in this multimillion dollar penthouse while parole officers fastened an ankle monitor to one of the tenants.

Sean shifted toward her, fast and unexpected. Their eyes met and she read it as a challenge. She wouldn't look away first.

"Want to order some Chinese food?" he asked.

That wasn't what she'd expected as his first words to her in "their new home." But she shrugged in agreement. *Hell, let him do whatever he wants.*

He pulled up a number on his phone while Harper dragged her laptop off the coffee table. She'd left it charging there last night, not knowing how much she'd want to disappear from sight as soon as she arrived with Sean.

She went through her email and opened the Craigslist jobs section while Sean listed off way too much food for two people. She'd missed that gravel in his voice, somehow incredibly sensual even when he did something as mundane as ordering Peking roasted duck.

Harper shifted as she snuck looks at him from over her laptop. Her mind might be in a rage at him and her heart might be on the verge of shattered, but her body was still highly attuned to him. *How can I hate someone so much and want them at the same time?*

Okay, maybe hate is a strong word. But still...

She nearly smiled when she saw an ad with the headline "Beautiful but broke?" *You got me*, she thought. Harper briefly wondered how desperate she'd need to be before she forayed into the adult entertainment industry. *Not that I really would,* she thought. But in that moment, Sean had turned her on so much by doing nothing but ordering dinner. It had been three weeks since they'd last been together, and before that she'd grown quite accustomed to mindblowing sex on a regular basis. *If I could just feel him one more time—*

"What are you doing?" His gruff voice briskly pulled her back to reality.

"Oh," she blushed and wondered if he could tell when she was wrapped up in a fantasy. "Looking for a job."

"A job? Like a new campaign?"

"Like a real job because I got fired," she shot back.

He blinked, and for a moment she wondered if it was the reaction she'd always feared. *Is he disgusted by me now that I'm not a model? Is that downward glance really trying to gauge how fat I've gotten?*

"Fucking idiots," he said. "Why the hell would they fire you? When did it happen?"

"When did it happen? Oh, I don't know. Sometime when you were in jail. I can't recall the exact date, considering it was sometime in the past *month*."

He looked hurt, but pressed on. "Come on, I really want to know. If I can help—"

"Help? How about this for some help? If you really want to know, I was on the way to tell you the fucking day you got arrested! Okay? That's when it happened."

"Oh."

"Yeah. Oh. Sorry my little nothing news was eclipsed by all your drama."

"Harper, I'm sorry. I truly am. I ... I don't know how else to say it."

She looked at him for a long pause. For a second, she almost gave in. *Just tell him it's okay.* She knew he'd take her back, at least momentarily, and she was so exhausted from being so scared, so angry.

But it's not okay, she reminded herself. There was an ocean of a chasm between them that couldn't be pieced back together. *At best, we have a hell of a mess to figure out.* She didn't know if she could ever really see him the same again.

Harper snapped her laptop closed and stood up. "Goodnight," she said.

"But what about dinner?" She let his voice get cut off by the slam of her bedroom door.

5

SEAN

He pinned her down. His large hand easily encircled her slender wrists. Bound by his flesh, Harper looked up at him through thick lashes. Sean's hardness pressed against the creamy skin of her upper thigh. The more he clenched his hand around her wrists, the more he sensed any trepidation in her vanish. She looked at him with total trust as she spread her legs wider.

She parted her lips to say something, but his other hand covered her mouth firmly. "Did I tell you to speak?" he asked.

Harper shook her head gently and he slid his length into her. Her center was familiar, warm and wet. Her eyes widened as he pressed against her G-spot and she let out a muffled cry beneath his hand.

As he began his rhythm into her, the juices that flowed were unbelievable. "How do you get so fucking wet?" he asked her. Sean lifted his hand briefly for her reply.

"You," she gasped in a small voice. "You do this to me."

He reclamped his hand over her mouth as she wrapped those long legs around his torso. Harper pulled him deeper with every thrust. The muscles of her thighs begged him to stay buried inside her.

He looked down to her breasts, the nipples hard and bright pink beneath him. As he released her wrists to lower his head to her breasts, the bedroom door shot open.

"LAPD," the officer boomed. Sean looked up as Harper cried out. He felt her come and her nails, free from his bind, dug into his back.

"Mom?" he asked.

It seemed only mildly unnatural that it was his mother commanding a squad of two other officers. Her always perfectly coifed hair fanned out from below the shiny vinyl cap.

"What do you think you're doing?" his mother asked. She reached for her baton, but pulled out a small silver flask instead. The other officers skirted the room, but he couldn't tear his eyes away from his mother, who guzzled the flask greedily.

"Fucking bitch—" Sean unwound himself from Harper and shot out of bed toward his mother, but as soon as his feet hit the floor she grew to the size of a monster.

"Why don't you go play with your brother?" his mom asked. She looked suddenly younger, the police uniform completely disappeared. It wasn't that she'd grown, but he'd shrunk. His childhood home, back on the East Coast, offered a perspective he hadn't seen in over twenty years. The tables, the wainscoting, the mahogany bar that hugged the wall, they were all adult-sized. Sean looked down to see a small pair of loafers on his feet. He'd always hated those loafers.

"Mama?" he said. The voice sounded tiny, small and scared.

His mother leered at him, draped across the wingback chair that curled against the bar. She took another long sip, still from a flask. He wondered where her favorite cut crystal tumbler was.

Far away, an alarm began to buzz. His mother and his childhood home faded to black. Sean's eyes shot open and he reached instinctively for Harper. The other side of his bed was cold.

As he pushed himself up, his hardness ached against the boxer shorts. The sheets were tangled and damp with his sweat. Beneath him, the mattress pushed back uncomfortably. It was still too new, too hard. *These dreams have to stop*, he thought to himself. It was too much, dreaming about a girl who was just on the other side of the penthouse. He heard the alarm fade in Harper's bedroom and the familiar traipse of her feet as she went to her en-suite.

Sean pulled on a pair of flannel pajama bottoms and adjusted himself in his boxers. He listened for Harper, but heard nothing. *Hopefully she'll hide herself in that bathroom for awhile.* The soundproofing of the largely concrete penthouse made it easy to live together, yet apart. Most of the time, except for her damn alarm, he couldn't hear her at all unless he really tried.

He snuck out of his bedroom toward the kitchen for a glass of water. His throat was tight and dry. *I gotta remember to keep a glass in the bathroom,* he thought. It would mean less chances of running into her—and getting turned on in the process.

As he turned the corner into the gourmet kitchen, he saw her standing barefoot before the fridge. A long, messy red braid snaked down her back. *It's just begging to be played with,* he thought. *Yanked, used to control and direct her.* When she reached for something in the fridge, her oversized t-shirt rose up those porcelain thighs. Any higher, and he'd get a glimpse of what was underneath. If anything at all.

He thought he could make out the bare triangle of her center, and his cock responded with an instant rehardening. Sean shifted and Harper spun around. Her eyes were like saucers, as big as they were in his dream. She clutched a jug of orange juice with an expression like she'd been caught doing something naughty. "Hey," she said, though her voice broke.

Sean didn't respond. He held her gaze while he opened three cupboards in search of the glasses. *Fucking Connor and his impossible idea of organization.* Finally, he found a glass and filled it with tap water.

"Do you want filtered water?" she asked. She watched him warily and scrambled for words to ease the silence. "We have some—"

"Chocolate," he said.

"What?" She cocked her head at him.

"Is there any chocolate?"

"Uh, yeah. I think so." She went to the pantry and rustled around. He watched her strong thighs as she bent and stretched. Harper examined the unfamiliar contents while Sean adjusted himself on one of the barstools.

"Cadbury," she said. She put a small box of imported chocolates on the marble waterfall island.

"Thank god. Not that American shit," he said. Sean picked up the solid milk chocolate bar, nearly impossible to find outside of Europe. He tore into the foil package and broke off a glossy square. As he placed it on his tongue to melt, he held out the bar to her.

"No thanks, I—"

"Have a piece," he said. She obliged without putting up a fight. However, he saw calculations flash across her eyes.

"Oh my god," she said. Harper closed her eyes as the rich British chocolate spread across her palate. "This is amazing."

"You've never had European chocolate before," he said. It was a statement, not a question.

"Well. Not unless you count Cadbury eggs," she said. "And that was years ago, as a child."

"They count," he said. "They're just not the best."

They both savored the chocolate in silence. Sean became aware of the slight hum of the refrigerator. Harper's face was bare without a whit of makeup. *Had he ever seen her like that before?* He couldn't remember. It was easier to see the spray of freckles across her nose, and her eyes looked more open than usual without the eyeshadow, heavy liner and false lashes. She looked younger, more innocent. And that made the desire beneath the flannel stir once again.

"I better go," she said. Harper broke the silence and started to pad away with bare feet.

Sean watched her go, a pang of loneliness in his chest. *Is there any way we could make this work?* he wondered.

He didn't know. There were all kinds of what ifs. What if he'd called her when he was in jail? How mad would she have been? Maybe she would have forgiven him instantly, soothed by the idea that she'd been one of the first people he reached out to.

He'd heard the stories. Supposedly, women loved it when a man showed his vulnerability. Vulnerability. It enraged him to even think of the word. He'd never needed anyone, so what could Harper have done?

Maybe it would have been different if she hadn't seen him shitfaced and getting arrested. It was impossible to erase something like that from your memory. And he didn't even know how bad it had been. *But it couldn't have been pretty*, he told himself. Years ago, with Ashton, an acquaintance had filmed one of their drunken nights. Sean hadn't realized it at the time, but when they'd been shown the video the next day he was immediately ashamed. Even in his drunken haze at the time, he'd been straight enough to realize he'd made an ass of himself.

On top of everything, he'd established himself with Harper as her dom. That meant he was her protector, always keeping his cool. The trust he'd broken by losing control like that, wailing on a cop, was probably irreparable.

Sean sighed and downed the last of the water. He opened the steel dishwasher to put the glass away, but thought better of it at the last moment. Instead, he left it on the island. It was a token, a challenge. *Let's see who puts it away first.*

As he made his way back to his bedroom, a pinch radiated from his ankle. *That damn ankle monitor.* Nobody talked about how fucking uncomfortable they were. It had already started to dig into his skin.

He thought about inching a sock up between his flesh and the monitor, but ditched the idea. *Hell, let it chew me raw if it wants. I deserve it.* As he lay in bed, he understood for the first time why some people cut. To feel something, anything, and let some of those overwhelming emotions release into the world. He hoped the ankle monitor would cut clean through him. At least it would give the police something to grimace about when it finally came off.

Sean closed his eyes and listened hard for any sounds of Harper in the penthouse. But he heard nothing. He strained as hard as he could until sleep finally reclaimed him.

6

HARPER

*H*arper ran her tongue along her teeth to pick up any remaining granules of sugar while she clicked through page after page of classifieds. She hadn't heard a peep from Sean since the strange encounter that morning. *What do you expect? It's not like he can go anywhere.* She'd probably sleep the day away, too, if she was housebound with no financial worries.

She went from Craigslist to Searchtempest and finally started scrounging through the local papers' online listings. When she'd first started her search, she'd adamantly only looked for listings adjacent to modeling. Now, she filtered for any reasonable key phrase from "fashion house" to "art gallery" and "designer."

It hadn't taken long for her to write off the major job search sites. Whenever she'd find a good fit, she'd spend thirty minutes completing a time-consuming form only to get an auto-response email of, "Thank you for submitting your resume! All positions have been filled, but we'll keep your application on file for future consideration."

Clearly, these so-called employers were simply hoarding resumes for leverage and data. Harper sighed as she hit submit on the eleventh application of the day. Immediately, a series of red warnings popped up. "Please correct the entries." *Fuck. If you don't do the formatting just how they want it, the whole thing is a bust.*

Harper rubbed her eyes, but every time she closed them images of Sean appeared. The last two days, ever since move-in, he'd consumed her thoughts. It hadn't helped seeing his bulging erection through the pajama pants that morning, either. She'd felt his eyes on her bare legs before he'd made a sound. Harper had intentionally lingered longer at the refrigerator than necessary in hopes that he would take her from behind.

Stop it. You need to focus on yourself right now. And your drastically dwindling bank account. It was almost too cozy, this current situation. Connor and Sam told her over and over that she was doing all of them, Sean included, a favor. But it didn't feel that way. Not paying any rent, any bills, and being showered with bedding, kitchenware and other basics kind of felt like the most awkward arranged marriage ever.

Except you're not sleeping with the other half, and he's got an ankle monitor strapped to him.

"Get it together, Harper," she told herself. "Any idiot can get a job." She'd toyed with the idea of entry-level positions. A lot of models waitressed on the side, even when they were booking shows and campaigns. She knew a lot of money could be made in tips if you looked good and flirted, but she knew she'd be a disastrous waitress. More importantly, she didn't want to be around food nonstop. The temptation would be too much.

Her calendar popped up with a reminder. "Pay Chase credit card." *Shit. What's the minimum payment on this one going to be?*

Harper opened the calendar to click on the link and saw another, standing reminder that she hadn't scheduled as a pop-up. "Aunt Flow." It was marked for yesterday.

Wait. My period was supposed to start yesterday? A flurry of panic rushed through her, but she tried to push it aside. It was normal for her to miss periods or not get them at all—one of the few good side effects of having such low body fat. But for the past few months, she'd been fairly regular. She hadn't liked to dwell on that since it was a clear reminder of how fat she'd become.

Stress can stop it, too, she reminded herself. Besides, Connor had commented when he'd moved her in that she was looking "thinner than usual." That compliment had given her a glow that had lasted for hours. It had been awhile since she'd weighed herself. Maybe she was finally back to her goal weight. *Thanks to Sean and his nonstop drama,* she thought.

Harper's phone lit up with a text. *Hey, whore,* P wrote. *Come out tonight! Industry party and I have a +1. Oodles of potential bosses for you to win over.*

An industry party. P had dragged her to some before. They were ridiculous affairs where half the partygoers donned leather assless chaps and not much else. Still, the leather, kink and adult industries had money, that was certain. She just didn't want to get propositioned nonstop to be a "new leading lady" like last time.

You have your read receipts on, bitch, P texted. *I know you're there.*

Sorry, I have to decline, she said. *Not feeling good.*

It was partially true. Her stomach had been feeling iffy, but she'd written it off as stress and the sudden surge of sugar from the chocolate square. It had to have at least 150 calories, it was so rich. The last thing she needed was a night of boozing with P.

Boo. Hit me up if you change your mind, grandma, P said.

She couldn't get the thought of that chocolate square out of her head. Not counting it—though of course she did—if she could make it to tomorrow morning, that would be two days of not eating. Add in the occasional squeeze of lemon to her water, that might make up twenty calories, tops.

Harper opened her food log, a simple spreadsheet. She'd tried apps and sites before, but didn't trust them to have the correct calorie and carb count. A lot of them didn't even have her special diet foods like zero-calorie organic condiments, so she'd waste time manually entering the information. *Why do their job for them?*

A spreadsheet was definitely better, and it didn't come with those pop-up warnings that she was "not consuming adequate nutrition for her age, gender and height." *Fucking morons.*

Harper scanned the calorie log. So far this week, she was under 900 calories per day. *How much, exactly, was that square?* She could sneak out to the pantry to peek at the wrapper, but that ran the risk of seeing Sean.

Instead, she Googled it and found the nutrition section on the official Cadbury site. With 240 calories per bar, how many squares total was it? Maybe six, that sounded right, but she'd better calculate for four just in case. That was sixty calories. Not nearly as bad as she'd thought, but not good either. It wasn't worth the calorie currency, and it was loaded with sugar and carbs.

Besides that goddamned chocolate, all the other foods that week had been in alignment with her standards. Half a turkey burger, one-quarter of a banana immediately before a cardio session, and those 70-calorie Boca burgers with 13 grams of protein each. All fuel for her workouts and helped to keep some muscle mass. She didn't need breasts that sagged. A little muscle, just a smidge, helped.

It wouldn't take much to work off those 60 calories. Harper jumped up and pulled on her Lululemons and a tight, moisture-wicking tank top. The downstairs gym wasn't particularly grand, but it had everything she needed.

Harper quietly snuck out of her room and jammed her feet into her Nikes at the door. Sean emerged from his room like he'd been waiting for her. "Where are you going?" he asked.

"Uh, the gym," she said.

"Your gym, the LA Fitness?" he asked.

She considered lying to him. Or actually going there, but then remembered her gas was nearly on empty. "No, just downstairs," she said.

"Wait, I'll go with you," he said.

She frowned as he closed the door to change. *Since when are you so modest?*

When he reappeared, he was in blue jersey shorts and a faded university t-shirt. With a cap tucked onto his head, he looked like a college boy. One with impressive muscles.

They took the stairs at her request. Harper had read that walking downhill and down flights of stairs were some of the best things you could do for bone mineral density. However, she felt his eyes on her ass the entire time and put an extra switch in her step.

She immediately climbed onto the elliptical, thankful it was in the corner. Harper switched off the wall-mounted television, and the black screen became a mirror that let her spy on the gym space behind her.

As she watched him warm up on the treadmill for ten minutes before switching to the free weights, her heart rate peaked. Not even the interval hill settings on the elliptical could fire her up so easily.

In the reflective screen, she watched him recline the bench to a forty-five degree angle and start his chest presses. A sheen of sweat gathered at his neck and made the raven tattoo look alive. For a moment, she forgot about how disgusting she was, how weak she was for that chocolate, and tried to just focus on not soaking through her yoga pants at the sight of him.

Sean sat up, whipped off his shirt, and switched to seated shoulder raises. *Goddamn.* Harper looked at the timer. Twenty-five minutes. Just five minutes more, and that would be enough—then she could race upstairs and take care of herself. If she could just get herself off with that image of Sean in her head, maybe it would straighten everything out.

When the elliptical hit the thirty-minute mark, she turned it off. Sean appeared beside her like a shark circling its prey. "Want to get lunch?" he asked. He didn't look at her face. Instead, he made no attempt to hide the fact that he was taking in her body. She blushed as his gaze skimmed across her crotch, and willed herself not to look and check if the violet pants had turned a deep purple at her center.

"No," she said brusquely and hopped off the machine. *No way was he going to force more food down her throat.*

"Are you sure? You were going pretty hard on that machine."

She turned crimson at the words.

"You need to feed your muscles after you work them," he said.

"Okay! Fine," she said. *Great. I just worked off that chocolate, and for what?*

They went up the stairs in silence, Harper skipping every other step for a little extra workout.

"Meet you out here in twenty," he called to her as she shut her bedroom door.

Any horniness she'd harbored was long gone by the time she peeled off her workout clothes.

Living together made hiding anorexia and bulimia a lot trickier. She was going to have to up her game if she was going to keep this secret buried.

7

SEAN

He picked at the raw, vegan roll while he watched the passersby. Sean knew he was lucky to have the little shop in the condo complex nestled on the first floor. He'd watched his ankle monitor carefully when he raced from the tenant entrance to the shop. It never even blipped. Although it was a tiny taste of freedom, it felt like a lot. Here, he could bring his laptop and work, get overpriced groceries, and even order from the tiny café. It usually sold out of everything save these inedible wraps, but he'd take what he could get.

Sean couldn't get over "lunch" yesterday with Harper. They'd discovered this café together, and he thought he'd seen disappointment in her face when she realized he could access the shop with his ankle bracelet.

Harper had quickly picked up a packet of seaweed, some sashimi and a bottle of no-sugar protein milk. "That's all?" he'd asked. "It's kind of ... a weird lunch."

"What's so weird about it?" she'd snapped. "It's Asian. A lot of people have sushi and seaweed."

He'd shrugged. "Just not what most people crave after a workout."

They'd taken the food back upstairs yesterday and eaten in near silence at the kitchen island. He'd watched her wrinkle her nose as she tipped the container of seaweed to one side.

"What?" he'd asked as he'd dug into his own meal of packaged peanut butter sandwiches.

"Look at all that oil," she'd said. "And it's full of sesame seeds."

"That's what gives it any semblance of flavor at all."

"I don't like it," she'd said. Harper had pulled out some chopsticks from the plastic baggie and picked at the food like it was a science experiment.

Now, Sean forced down the vegan wrap between generous dips in soy sauce. At least the smoothies they whipped up were on point. Thick with extra scoops of whey powder for extra protein. This would be his one and only reprieve from the coldest co-living situation ever.

"Sean?"

He looked up and peered over his open laptop. It took him a minute to remember their names. "Eli, Manny, what are you guys doing here?" he asked.

"Post-workout smoothies," Eli said. "Man, we haven't seen you since ... well—"

"Since the accident," Sean said. "I know." He was used to those looks and those long pauses. Nobody seemed to know how to handle talking about the night his friend had gone into a coma.

"We heard Ashton's better now," Manny piped up. His round, brown face glistened with sweat. "I mean, kind of."

"What's that mean?" Sean asked.

Eli and Manny approached Sean's table with low voices. They'd been tertiary party friends, but never went as hardcore as Sean and Ashton. Still, Sean had glimpses of some nights with the four of them at rooftop parties and sharing bottle service.

"I mean … he's already addicted again, man," Manny said. "I don't know, I shouldn't talk. It's just what people are saying."

"People? What people? Addicted to what?"

"People like the guy we get our party favors from," Eli said. "I mean, he wasn't overt about it or anything. Just said something like, 'Ashton said it was for all of you' when we showed up to get a little molly."

"Yeah, then kind of gave us shit about girly party drugs. That's what he called it."

"So, what's Ashton on?" Sean asked. *Why do you care?*

"I dunno, man. I heard it was like coke and some kind of scripts. You know, the usual LA shit. You haven't heard any of this?" Eli asked.

"No. Honestly, I've been kind of …" he trailed off, unsure how much to tell them. Or how much they knew. *It's not exactly smart to go around advertising that you punched a cop or were in jail.*

"Hey, what's that?" Manny asked. He pointed to Sean's ankle.

Fuck. "Uh, an ankle monitor," he said.

"For real? What for? The whole Ashton thing? Man, that's bullshit—"

"No," he said quickly. "Not really. I uh, kind of got into an altercation a couple of weeks ago. With a cop."

"No shit!" Eli looked impressed. His eyes lit up. "What'd you do?"

"Punched him," Sean said with a shrug. "I'd been drinking, they showed up at my place, you know how it goes."

"Fucking A, man," Eli said. He shook his head in wonder. "You're my hero, you know that?"

"Yeah. It's not really awesome to be wearing this for the next however long," Sean said.

"So, wait. How are you here then?"

"I live here."

"What?" Manny looked impressed. "In this building? Man, I saw this when I was looking for some new digs. It was crazy expensive even then. You've got some serious tricks up your sleeve, Sean."

"Something like that," he said. "Hey, I gotta get going," he said. He hoped, desperately, that they wouldn't ask him where. It wasn't like he had that many options.

"Okay, cool," Eli said. "You still got the same number? I'll hit you up. Or just text me whenever your anklet gets off."

"Sounds good," Sean said. "Later."

He grabbed his laptop, shoved it in his bag and made a beeline for the tenant entrance.

As he took the elevator to the penthouse, he couldn't help but reflect on everything that had happened. It wasn't that long ago that he'd been in that car with Ashton, but it felt like a different person. A different life.

Those days of hardcore partying, of waking up with piles of naked women in his bed whose names he couldn't remember, what the hell had he been doing? And Eli and Manny, what kind of assholes were impressed with an ankle monitor?

He hung the bag on the bronze hooks as he stepped inside. Harper's door was closed as usual, but he saw a dim light from below the door.

Sean sighed as he filled a glass of water. Even now, in this apartment chosen by his brother with the monitor hugging his leg, he was so much closer to where he wanted to be than ever before. He had Joon-ki with his endless patience. Even though he'd started off as his sponsor, the relationship had quickly turned to genuine friendship. *Joon-ki's the kind of person you need in your life,* he told himself as he downed the water. *Eli and Manny weren't the ones waiting for you at the jailhouse, were they?*

And Harper. God, he was lucky to have her. *Not that you have her anymore,* he reminded himself. But she was here. She'd given up her entire life to help him out. Even after everything she'd seen. Even after everything he'd put her through.

Harper fulfilled every fantasy he'd ever had, and even those he hadn't fully accepted until she came into his life. Sean had always imagined that if he found the right sub, the right sexual fit, he could compartmentalize. He could keep his sub at arm's length, on call for his whims, and that would be it. Harper broke through those molds. She was the ultimate

Madonna-whore, and he was infatuated with every facet of her.

And then there was the job. Connor hadn't spoken to him much about it since he'd bailed him out beyond a single whisper during move-in. "The job's still yours if you want it." Sean had looked at him with utter surprise. Who would keep a drunk on board, even if it was their brother?

But Connor had just grinned, slapped Sean's back and shook his head. "We'll talk later," he'd said.

In fact, it was somewhat perfect timing. Connor was taking a hiatus from opening the business for paternity leave. As Sam got closer to her due date, reality set in harder. The last he'd heard, they both planned to take at least three months off post-baby, before making the move to California and opening up shop.

A lot can happen in three months, Sean thought. Harper was proof of that. Three months ago, he'd been toiling away in the tattoo shop. Then one day, she'd just appeared, asking for that lower back snake tattoo with her idiotic friends.

You never know when your life's about to change. For better or worse. He hadn't seen Harper coming, but he hadn't seen that night with Ashton coming, either.

"Jesus, Ashton," he whispered to himself. *How could he just go back to the same old lifestyle? Did he really think it was all on Sean, what had happened that night?* "I wasn't even driving," Sean said. He'd said it so many times, but it was like nobody listened. He wasn't the druggie, he hadn't been snorting blow all night, he hadn't had god knows how many pills. Why had it all come down on him?

He felt bad for Ashton. For the first time, he felt compassion and empathy without a trace of guilt. No matter what anyone said, once Ashton was out of that coma all decisions were on him. It was proof for Sean he hadn't been at fault that night.

And now there was Harper. He looked to the closed door and the warm light that trickled onto the concrete floors. He had to make up with her, one way or another. Or at least try. Sean had never felt this way about anyone before.

Besides, they lived together. As odd and unorthodox as the situation was, that had to be a sign. And it gave him an advantage, that closeness. How hard could it be?

8

HARPER

*H*arper wavered at the coffee table. In a peace offering gesture, she'd steeped tea for both of them. However, as she leaned over the steaming pot, it poured into her head and made the room spin.

"Are you okay?" Sean asked. He reached forward from the couch to steady her.

"I don't—"

That was the last thing she remembered before darkness fell over her. She had just enough sense and stamina to aim toward the soft sheepskin rug instead of the hard floors. Sean's voice sounded far away as he called out for her.

She felt pinching restraints against her forearms, which woke her up. "Sean?" she asked. "It's too tight … "

"Your husband couldn't come," a strange female voice said. "Don't worry, you'll be okay."

"Where … where am I?"

"Right now you're in an ambulance. We're taking you to St. Vincent." The woman was all business in her white uniform. Harper lifted her head to look at her arms, but was immediately, gently, pushed back down. "You're okay, sweetie," the woman said. "We just strapped you in for cautionary measures."

"What happened?" Harper asked.

"Your husband said that you fainted."

"He's not my husband."

"Okay, well your boyfriend or roommate or whoever called 9-1-1. He said you fainted and he couldn't wake you up. Has this ever happened before?"

Harper considered how much to tell them. *Of course I've fainted before, I'm a model.* Get hungry enough, and your body will just shut down temporarily. But she'd never been out for that long. She'd only fainted a few times, but every time she was almost immediately alert again. "I don't know," she said finally.

"Okay. Have you had any head injuries lately? A concussion?"

"No," she said, happy to be blunt and honest.

"Is there any possibility you could be pregnant?"

"I don't ... I don't know."

"Alright. Don't worry, we're almost there. We have your purse here, is your insurance information in there?"

"It should be," she said. Harper couldn't bring herself to admit to this stranger that she'd let it lapse. *Screw it, you've already racked up an ambulance bill. How much would that be, a thousand dollars?*

The familiar street names and lights looked alien from this reclined angle. "Why aren't the sirens on?" she asked.

"That's only for emergencies."

At least you're not an emergency. Maybe that would lower the bill a little. When the ambulance pulled up to the ER entrance, the driver raced around back to help. "I can walk," Harper said, suddenly embarrassed at the attention. Even as patients limped into the ER, they stared openly at the scene she'd created.

"Sorry, that's not allowed."

She squeezed her eyes shut as she was wheeled into the bright fluorescent hallway. There was no stopping at reception or filling out of forms. Apparently when you arrived via ambulance, you got the full star treatment.

Harper was wheeled into a small exam room. Down the hall, she could hear the screams and belligerent cries of her fellow patients. It felt like an hour before a nurse finally came in. "Harper, my name is Joy. I'm just going to take down some information, get your vitals, and the doctor will be in as soon as she can, okay?"

"Okay." Harper knew it was the middle of the day, but she was exhausted. She was on autopilot as she answered the nurse's questions.

"Is the address on your license correct?"

"Um, no. I just moved. I … I don't remember the address."

"That's okay, we can update it later."

God. You don't even know where you live.

"Who should we put down as an emergency contact?"

"Sean Harris." His name was out of her mouth before she could register it. *Was he really the first one she thought of?* She even knew his number by heart.

"Okay, now I'm going to check your blood pressure, lungs, and draw some blood. Huh," the nurse said. "Such slender arms. I'm jealous! Hold on, I'll need to get a children's cuff for this."

Harper smiled into the fluorescent light. *You're not fat*, she beamed to herself. *A children's cuff!*

"Alright, that's better," the nurse said. The cuff looked so much less serious than the big, bulky black one—so big, Harper simply couldn't fill it. "That's ... one-sixty over one-ten. Do you have a history of high blood pressure in your family? That's pretty high for someone your age and weight."

"I think it's just stress," Harper said. *Idiot.* She'd lost count of how many times doctors and medical professionals were stumped by her strange numbers. *Don't you know being so thin gives you high blood pressure? Don't they teach you that in medical school?*

"Could be," the nurse said. "I'll just make a note of it. You'll want to follow up on that if it continues."

Yeah, that's what I want to spend my no-insurance money on. Monitoring a so-called condition when I know perfectly well what the cause is.

"And now the blood," the nurse said. "Do needles bother you?"

She almost laughed. "No," she said. *Needles are what brought me to Sean.*

"Okay," the nurse said. "All done! We're pretty busy today, but the doctor will be in as soon as she can. Just sit tight."

She dozed off even with the blinding lights. The gut-wrenching sobs of children worked their way into her dreams. Punctuated by the sounds of messy technical jargon, she dreamed of her childhood home and the time she'd split her lip open when she ran smack into the doorframe.

"Harper! What are you doing?" her mom had rushed to her while Harper's best friend from kindergarten was frozen with an open mouth. The taste of blood, coppery, filled her mouth.

She'd started to cry, not from the pain, but for the attention and for the sheer wildness of it all.

"I … I …" she'd stammered.

"What the hell happened?" her mom had exclaimed and turned on her friend.

"We … we were playing tag, and she …"

"Harper!" her mom had said as she turned back to her. She examined the lip. "Do you know this might scar? Do you know how important your face is?"

A girlish scream pierced her brain. "You're scaring the other patients," a stern voice said. Her mom was gone and a bright light flooded through her eyelids.

Harper felt a firm, warm hand on her forearm. Her eyes fluttered open. A pretty Indian woman with tired black eyes looked down at her. "Sorry to disturb your sleep," she said. "I'm Dr. Chatterjee."

"Oh. Hi," Harper said, her voice thick with sleep.

"Well, Harper, we have a few things to discuss."

I'm dying, she thought ridiculously. "What, uh ... what's wrong with me?"

"If you mean why did you faint, I have a couple of theories. For one, you're severely dehydrated. We'll be getting a tube in you immediately to address that."

"A tube? Not like a feeding tube, right? I mean, it's just water ..."

The doctor looked at her curiously. "Why would you ask about a feeding tube?"

Harper blushed. "I don't know, I'm sorry. I'm still kind of out of it—"

"Harper," the doctor said gently. "I see a lot of models and actresses. This is LA. I know it's trendy right now to dehydrate yourself to get that toned look all the time now, not just for photo shoots. But it's dangerous. Especially for someone in your condition."

"My condition?"

"You ... you do know you're pregnant, right?"

"What? How do you know? That can't be—"

"It came back in the blood test. We can retest, but blood work is very accurate."

"Please don't tell anyone," Harper said urgently. She grasped for the woman's hands. "Please."

"Harper, you're a grown woman. And there's doctor-patient confidentiality. I don't intend to tell anyone, nor is it legal for me to do so. But ... are you alright? I can have a nurse refer you to some pregnancy support organizations. All unbiased and many free or on a sliding scale."

"Okay," Harper said. Anything to shut the woman up. *How can I be pregnant?*

"Do you want me to call someone for you? Your emergency contact?"

"No!" Harper said immediately. "No. Thank you. I ... my phone should be in my purse. I'll take care of it."

"If you're sure," the doctor said. "We do need to keep you here for awhile. Partially for observation, and partially to get your hydration levels back up. I'd also recommend you talk to one of the nutritionists on staff."

"Nutritionists?"

"I can't tell you much with just the blood work, but in my experience dehydration in a woman your age often goes hand in hand with malnutrition. It's often an attempt to fit a certain mold of what women are supposed to look like. Given your height and bone structure ... are you a model?"

"Was," Harper said glumly.

"I know how demanding that industry can be," the doctor said. "And I know what lengths women in that profession go to in order to maintain their figure. No matter what you decide to do about the pregnancy, I want you to meet with a nutritionist before you're discharged."

"Fine," Harper said. She forced a smile at the doctor, the looked away until the woman exited through the curtain.

She dug her phone out of her purse. It was full of missed calls and texts from Sean. *Hey*, she texted. *I'm okay, just getting fluids at the hospital.*

What's wrong? What happened?? Sean texted.

Her phone lit up with a call, which she silenced. *Can't talk now, nurses coming in,* she said. *Just dehydrated, that's all. Should be released in a few hours.*

Call me when you can? Sean asked.

Ok. Putting phone on airplane mode now to save battery.

She turned off the phone and closed her eyes.

What the fuck are you going to do now? she thought.

9

SEAN

As soon as Harper pulled up to the building in a cab, Sean opened the glass doors to usher her in. He couldn't read her expression behind the huge sunglasses she must have dug out of her purse. "Are you alright?" he asked.

She waved him away after she'd taken the rolled-up twenty out of his hand and handed it to the driver.

"Don't run!" he'd called after her as she hurried back to the waiting yellow taxi.

"I'm fine," she huffed. Harper stiffened and pulled away from his hand on her lower back, but she didn't actively shoo him away.

"We're taking the elevator," he said when she veered toward the stairs. She opened her mouth to protest but snapped it shut again.

He held the door open for her and she pulled off the sunglasses. A dark ring had settled in beneath each eye.

"What's with all the blankets?" she asked.

Sean looked to the couch. Maybe he had gone overboard. It was piled high with all the extra blankets and pillows he could find—and considering Sam had gone above and beyond when furnishing the loft, there were plenty to be had. "I just wanted you to be comfortable."

"I have a bed where I can be comfortable," she said.

"No arguing. Get on the couch and I'll make you some soup."

"I'm not sick! I was just dehydrated—"

"All the more reason to have some soup."

He set up Netflix to stream on the television and was pleased when he saw her begrudgingly dismantle the pile of blankets and pillows to hole up on the couch.

The little shop hadn't had much variety with the soup, so he'd bought one of each flavor. He peeled open the chicken noodle soup, poured it in one of the white bowls, and started the microwave.

"What's this?" she asked. Harper wrinkled her nose at it.

"Chicken noodle soup."

"Great. Pasta in a broth."

"Just eat what you can," he said. *God, she was an annoying sick person.* His phone buzzed in his pocket. "It's my lawyer, I have to take this," he said. She waved him away as she carefully scooped just broth into the spoon.

"Hi," he said quietly as he slipped away to his bedroom. "Please tell me you have good news."

"Actually, I do," T said. "It turns out the police officer you punched is letting you off the hook."

"What? He's not pressing charges?"

"Nope. Although, honestly it's probably because his ego is bruised and he doesn't want to waste time with all the paperwork and court time. LAPD has bigger fish to fry than you."

"Uh, thanks? I guess," he said.

"Just being honest. Here's some more good news to cheer you up, all the other charges have been lowered to misdemeanors."

"All of them?" Sean's heart swelled, but he didn't want to get too excited yet.

"All of them," T repeated. "Once again, I think it's the court's lack of time and money to pursue them, not that the assault charge has been dropped. The other charges were kind of banking on that as a catalyst."

"That great!" Sean said. "But what exactly does a misdemeanor mean?"

"Well, that's the tricky part," T said. "They come with a relatively hefty fine, though I get the sense that's not a huge barrier for you."

Sean stayed silent, waiting for the bomb to drop.

"Anyway, the repercussions kind of depend on what you plan to do. It might impact future job prospects, professional licenses, and in the future, child custody. Technically, misdemeanors don't come with jail sentences most of the time, but you might go back to jail while we wait for everything to be resolved. That can be up to two months."

"But I'm on bail."

"That was only while we got to this part of the process," T

said. "At the moment, we're in limbo."

"Isn't there, I don't know, anything we can do? To get some of those dropped?"

T drew in a breath and Sean heard Harper laugh at something on the television. "Yes, actually," she said. "If you could talk Ashton into dropping the witness statement, we have a really good shot."

"Okay," he said. *Never gonna happen.* "Thanks."

"Sean! Let me know if you'll be able to talk to him by Friday, alright?"

"Yeah, will do," he said.

"You didn't ask about the last good news."

"There's more?"

"An officer will be by later today to remove your ankle monitor."

"That's it?" He was shocked. Sean had already grown accustomed to the bulky little appendage.

"That's it."

"Thanks. For everything," he said.

"That's what I'm here for."

"And, hey, one more thing?"

"Yes?"

"Could you maybe ... make an overture to Ashton for me? See if he'd even be willing to see me. I, I don't know. I have a feeling this isn't going to go over well. But now that I'll be able to leave the house soon, it's worth a shot."

"Definitely. I'll have someone in the office connect with him later today. This really is your best bet for coming out of this in the clear. You're lucky, you know that?"

"I have my doubts," he said. "Thanks again."

"No problem, you'll hear from me soon."

Sean sat on the edge of his bed and contemplated the situation with Ashton. No matter how many angles he tried, he couldn't seem to get anything to sound right. And judging by what Eli and Manny had said, it didn't sound like Ashton was in any kind of mood to be generous. He'd be lucky to talk to him when he wasn't totally coked out of his mind.

Finally, Sean emerged from the bedroom. He crept up quietly to the couch and found Harper sleeping. All the noodles and most of the chicken remained in the bowl, but it seemed like she'd spooned out all of the broth.

She looked tiny and gaunt curled up on the couch. Maybe that was to be expected after spending so many hours at the hospital. *I'll make her eat more. And better. I have to,* he thought to himself. Harper was beyond thin, even for a model. Her natural curves suggested a richness in her breasts and hips, but a lot of it was the natural splay of her bones. A touch of it was the small amount of muscle she put on at the gym, and she was simply blessed with those breasts.

Who are you to think you can handle this kind of restriction? He struggled with the word anorexia. *Was that what it was? When did someone cross the line from health-conscious to obsessed? To a mental disorder?*

Sean settled into the chair across from her. He remembered being a little boy and how his mother would sleep on the couch from noon onward, sluggish from alcohol. Eventually, she gave up the pretenses and went straight to bed after her lunchtime vodka.

Once, his father came home unexpectedly from a business trip. Sean was only seven years old, but he was aware of the sizzle in the air. His mother had been a semifunctional alcoholic, and had always arranged for the cleaners to arrive the day before his father returned. This time, she wasn't prepared.

The house was a disaster. He and Connor weren't quite old enough yet to be embarrassed. They reveled in the mess, at the idea that they could toss plates of snacks and their juices on the floor with zero repercussions.

For five days, their mother had only slumped out of the bedroom to go to the bathroom or refill her vodka. When their father walked in, he and Connor hadn't bathed in five days, either. They wore the same pajamas. He could still recall the stink of it.

It was summer, and neither had any responsibilities. Their father, with steely eyes, gently set his briefcase on the foyer table. "Where's your mother?" he asked them.

"In bed," Connor said quietly.

"How long has she been shut up in there?"

"I don't know..."

"How long, Connor?" his father boomed.

"Five days," he said meekly.

Their father surveyed the mess of the great room. Without a word, he stalked to the bedroom. The sound of his expensive shoes made a clip-clop sound like a horse at the races.

Sean expected to hear screaming, a glass shattering, the usual sounds of what happened behind their closed doors. But there was nothing.

Instead, their father appeared in the bedroom doorway. Their mother was passed out in his arms. She was beautiful, even in such a state, like a Hollywood actress in the arms of her leading man.

"Where are you taking Mom?" Connor said, suddenly fueled with fear. He jumped up and pulled uselessly at his father's arm. "Put her down!"

Their father kicked in his general direction until Connor gave up. "Knock it off, Connor, shit!" he yelled. "I'm taking her somewhere to rest for awhile. You both start cleaning up while I'm gone."

It wasn't until years later that Sean realized his mother had actually been taken to dry out. Those sessions never lasted long. She'd return, a clarity in her voice and eyes, and promise them over and over she was done drinking. "I just don't feel like it anymore!" she would coo.

It never took more than a couple of weeks until she was back at the bottle. In time, Sean came to see these dry outs as times of peace and quiet. Often, his father would jet off to another business trip and hire a nanny who didn't care what they did as long as they were quiet.

Still, his mother's drinking was never quite as bad as that time. He shook his head and looked at Harper. *Please don't let her be that far gone.*

He was pretty sure he could handle it, all of it. No matter how deep the eating disorder had wormed. *You just have to watch her.*

10

HARPER

The heat of the radiated floors warmed her from the bottom up. Harper stood barefoot in the kitchen, a cut of uncooked chicken breast on the butcher block. Her little food scale sat beside it. Just the look of the sickly, pale flesh made her nauseated. She hoped for a revulsion so thick it would make her vomit. *That would be nice, no cut-up knuckles for once.* Of course, it never came.

Harper held her breath as she put the chicken breast in a Ziploc bag and weighed it. One hundred grams. She'd have to cut off a small piece to get it down to an even 150 calories.

She grimaced as she snipped off a piece of the meat and reweighed. Harper didn't know if it was the pregnancy or the eating disorder that made this so difficult. *It's not like you haven't had chicken breast before.* White meat, relatively low calories, and all protein with no carbs. After shellfish, it was one of the best choices she could make.

"What am I doing?" she whispered aloud to the empty kitchen. She still didn't know what she'd do about the baby.

Why get attached to something that might not even survive? Her body was so fucked up, so malnourished, it wasn't exactly the ideal environment for new life.

It wasn't a surprise that so many celebrities had trouble conceiving. Why even young models opted for IVF or, better yet, surrogates. At 900 calories a day, she shouldn't even be able to sustain herself long-term—yet alone someone else.

It would be better to just get rid of it now, she told herself. What was it, the size of a peanut, if that? She could get over an abortion at this point. But at the second trimester? The third? A miscarriage at that point might do her in. Even though she was aware of the life within her, without any bumps or kicks, she could still play pretend.

"You busy?" Sean popped his head into the kitchen. He glanced briefly at the chicken breast in her hand. "I want to show you something. I mean, if you'll let me."

"No, what is it?" she asked, eager for an excuse to walk away from the chicken. She ran her hands under hot water and scrubbed briefly before she followed him.

"This way," he said over his shoulder.

She was uncertain as she followed him into his bedroom. *Now? This is how we're going to restart things?*

"Oh my god!" she gasped. "What is this?"

She didn't know when he'd done it, but the entire bedroom was lined in white butcher paper from floor to ceiling. The windows were covered and sunlight pushed through the paper. Every strip had a drawing of a person on it—and they were all her, each done in incredible detail. She'd forgotten how talented he was, how he took to human skin as canvas with a needle in his hand. About the stunning mural in his old, small apartment.

Harper went from drawing to drawing, each perfectly to scale. In some incarnations, she was dressed in one of the couture pieces she'd borrowed from her old housemate Molly. In others she was folded in a seated position, wearing her favorite wornout sweats. He'd depicted her both in full-blown glam makeup, and barefaced with a sloppy ponytail.

"I don't understand," she said. Harper shook her head as she traced the outline of one of her copies. He'd used various mediums from charcoal to acrylic paint and watercolors. Some of the pieces were still mildly damp.

She looked to him, but he just shrugged. There was no expression on his face. "I just want you to see yourself how I see you."

"This ... these are beautiful," she said.

"Exactly." She tried not to let him see how she compared herself to her standing figure. *Was her waist really that small?* It couldn't be. In the drawings, they seemed exaggerated, almost a caricature of an hourglass body. *This can't be right.* But as she sidled up close to it, she had to admit that the dimensions lined up.

"My calculations are perfect," Sean said.

She blushed, thankful that her back was to him. Even if he did get the measurements right, and it seemed he had, it was easy to gloss over flaws. Simple to exaggerate the few good qualities she had. *How could someone really see me like this?*

Harper continued along the wall until the images changed. Suddenly, Joon-ki stared back at her, his almond-shaped eyes warm and deep. "It looks just like him," she said.

"That's kind of the point."

"No, it's more than the details. You captured his essence in this." The creation was so lifelike, so spot on, she couldn't fathom how he could do it all from memory. There were elements of Joon-ki she would have never remembered herself until she saw them. How he had that tiny freckle below his right eye, nearly obscured by the black lashes.

"Who's this?" she asked, and her nose wrinkled when she came to a vaguely familiar figure. Then she saw the raven nestled in flowers on the figure's neck. "Is this supposed to be you?" She looked at him with curiosity.

"It is me," he said.

"No … this barely looks like you," she said. "I thought artists were supposed to be good at self-portraits." She walked along a series of so-called Sean images. But they were all wrong, off somehow. Most were far shorter than he was, and some were close to ugly. The eyes were too wide apart, the hairline too low, the royal nose squat and flat as a mushroom. "Is this how you see yourself?" she asked.

He gave her a curt nod.

She felt her heart crack and crumble into pieces. *I know how that feels,* she thought, but she couldn't get the words out. Instead, she circled back to the first images, the ones of her. The woman who stood before her was simultaneously familiar and a stranger. It was like one of those exaggerated caricatures you could get of yourself along the Seine in Paris. The artists only dared to highlight your ugly features if they thought you could handle it. For the most part, they picked the elements you might like about yourself and blew them up. *Was that what he'd done to her?*

But, no. She could see it wasn't a caricature. The woman who was represented before her was easily a real person. "Is this really how you see me?" she asked softly.

"Yes, but it's not just how I see you," he said. "It's how you really are. You have no idea how beautiful you are, do you?"

Tears threatened to spill down her cheeks. She wanted to tell him she both knew it and didn't. Obviously, there was something about her or she wouldn't have had such a successful career. She knew her height, the broad shoulders and unbelievably small waist were built not just for modeling, but for being a supermodel. She'd never fit in with the runway waifs who weighed eighty pounds without even trying. Once, a director had told her she should have been working during the heyday of the 1990s supermodels. Cindy Crawford, Naomi Campbell, that's who she was built like. But she'd started her career when heroin chic was in hot demand. And that was a skeletal ideal she could never fully attain. "Thank you for showing me," she told him. It was the most she could get out.

She turned to leave, but paused at the door. Her hand rested lightly on the thick wood trim painted a steely gray. Harper turned her head. "Do you know how to cook chicken?" she asked.

"Yeah," he said, surprised.

"I ... I have some. And some vegetables, but I think I can just steam those in the microwave. If ... if you're not busy, and you don't mind cooking—"

"Sure," he said. She sensed the eagerness below the surface, but for once she didn't care. She was in control. Everything she had for dinner had been hand-selected by her, so there wouldn't be any surprises. She could, she was allowed, to eat it all.

Besides, pregnant women are supposed to have more calories, she thought. There was some comfort in knowing the baby would gobble up the excess. However, more comforting was the idea that she was nourishing another living thing. A baby that was half her, half Sean.

She led them into the kitchen and gestured helplessly at the glob of pinkish meat on the counter.

"What are you doing to this poor thing?" Sean asked as he examined the cut-up breast and little sliver of discovered excess calories.

"I don't know," she said. There was no way she'd admit she had to weigh it all.

He shook his head in wonder and pulled out the remaining cuts of meat from the Styrofoam packaging. Sean rinsed the meat and put a pot over medium heat. She almost cried out when he drizzled some olive oil into the pan, but held it together. Olive oil had so many calories, and she didn't have a clue how much he'd used.

He glanced up at her. "Olive oil is good for you," he said.

"How come?"

"Good fats," he said. She hated that word. "Antioxidants, anti-inflammatory properties. It's supposed to help with preventing strokes, heart disease—"

"You make it sound like I'm eighty years old."

He shrugged. "If you waited until you're eighty to start taking care of your body, you probably wouldn't be in a very good position." Sean started to chop up a head of cauliflower.

"Maybe you're right." She picked at one of the pieces of cauliflower and chewed on the white blandness mindlessly.

"You might want something on that," Sean said. He smiled at her kindly. "Here, I'll show you."

11

SEAN

He woke up late, aware from the way the sun poured through the butcher paper that it was close to midday. Sean groaned and checked his phone. Almost eleven.

He hadn't heard Harper at all. Normally, he was woken up by her blending of smoothies in the morning for her pre-gym protein. Sean pulled himself out of bed and adjusted his morning erection. Already, dreams of the previous night escaped him, but he knew they had all been of Harper. They always were.

"Hey," he said as he opened his bedroom door. She was curled up on the couch. A book rested on her knees.

"Hi," she said. For once, the smile that spread across her face was easy and natural. It was the first time since they'd moved in together.

"You haven't eaten?" he asked.

She shook her head. "Not in the mood for a smoothie," she said.

"How about brunch?"

"Okay," she said.

He made his way to the kitchen. Yesterday, when she asked him to cook for her, it had been a sign. That was his way back to her. Sean pulled out a half-dozen eggs from the fridge and a packet of English muffins. He cracked the shells and started to whisk egg yolks with lemon juice in a stainless steel bowl for hollandaise sauce.

He heated a saucepan with a thin layer of water. As he drizzled in butter and watched the sauce thicken and double in size, he sensed Harper behind him. Afraid to say anything, worried that it might scare her away, he reached for the salt and cayenne.

"Are you making eggs benedict?" she asked.

"Yeah."

"I didn't know people actually made that."

He laughed as he started to brown bacon in a skillet. "Did you think they just appeared?"

"I don't know!" she said. He handed her two English muffins to toast. "I thought they were really hard to make. Like, only chefs made them."

"They're not hard," he said. He broke another egg into the water and reduced the heat to a simmer.

"How do you know when they're done?" she asked. Harper peered into the pan.

"Practice," he said.

"Thanks."

"About three and a half minutes," he said. "Watch for the egg white to set but the yolk should still be soft." He removed one of the eggs with a slotted spoon and let it drain over a paper towel. As he carefully assembled the benedict and spooned the poached egg on top of the bacon, he seasoned both plates with salt and pepper. Finally, with the hollandaise poured over them and a garnish of chopped parsley, he handed Harper her plate.

She looked at it like it was a science experiment. Sean could see numbers and calculations flying across her face. "Just try it," he said gently. "It's good for you."

He ushered her toward a seat at the kitchen island and kept an eye on her while he put more bacon into the pan and pulled out the pancake mix. "You're making more?" she asked, her eyes wide.

"You haven't had breakfast or lunch, have you?"

She didn't answer, but when he pushed the freshly cooked bacon onto her plate, she made a face and started blotting at the strips. "How many calories are in bacon?" she asked.

"Does it really matter? Just enjoy it."

She gave him a look like a surly teenager. He watched her as she nibbled on everything, going at the egg whites with more gusto than anything else. When the first batch of pancakes were done, he forked two onto her plate, but Harper shook her head vehemently. "No more," she said.

He sighed and looked at her plate. For her, she'd eaten a decent amount, though it still wasn't nearly enough to count as sustenance.

"You interested in working out together again?" she asked.

"I don't know. Maybe," he said. "It's Sunday. I thought maybe we could lounge on the couch and watch a movie first. We can decide if we want to work out later."

"Okay," she said reluctantly.

"Hey. How about you choose the movie?"

"Really?" she asked, brightening.

"Go on, I'll clean up."

Harper rushed to the living room while he rinsed the dishes and loaded the dishwasher. By the time he made it to the living room, she had *Mean Girls* cued up on Netflix.

"Seriously?" he asked.

"You said I could choose." She pulled a face that dared him to disagree.

They sat on opposite ends of the couch like armies readying for battle. Eventually, Harper propped her feet up on the couch, taking up two-thirds of it. "You want a foot rub?" Sean asked.

She looked startled, but bit her lip and nodded.

He started at her perfectly dainty feet, cold to the touch. Sean warmed them, surprised at the softness—especially with all the working out and those insanely high heels she wore. When he worked his way to her bare calves, she didn't react. The rolled-up boxers she wore as pajama bottoms had hiked up so high that his hands had miles of flesh to explore.

Sean reached her thigh and she squirmed. When he raised his eyes to hers, there was a hunger in there he hadn't seen in weeks. She lunged at him. Her lips met his as her arms snaked around his neck.

Without thinking, he kissed her back. Harper's hand twisted around the front of his t-shirt and she pulled him closer. That kind of desire, that dominance, was new in her. Any other time, he'd despise it, but something about it being her made him harden instantly.

Sean pulled off her tank top and yanked down her shorts. She wore no bra, no underwear, nothing. If he'd known the only thing that stood between him and her ethereal body were a few wisps of cotton, it would have been impossible to make it through brunch without bending her over the island and fucking her senseless.

He stood up and cradled her into his arms. Her mouth consumed his and she tugged at his shirt uselessly as he carried her to his bedroom. "No," he said as he tossed her onto the mattress. Her breasts bounced and her nipples hardened when she hit the black duvet.

Sean leaned over her and pinned her hands above her head with one hand. "You don't want to know what will happen if you move your hands. Understand?"

"Yes."

"Yes, what?"

"Yes, sir," she said.

He was hard as a rock, but the desire to taste her, consume her, overpowered everything else. Sean worked his way from her hungry mouth to the salt of her collarbone. He took one nipple between his lips and sucked while she writhed and moaned.

As he flicked his tongue across her abdomen, he caught a scent of her desire. Harper's legs were spread wide, eager, her clit already swollen with want.

He dipped his tongue into her wet folds and heard her cry out. Still, she kept her hands above her head in an invisible bind. For an hour, he teased her clit. She tried to grip his head with her thighs, to fuck his face while following his rules, but each time he'd firmly push open her thighs.

Sean refused to indulge in any pleasure for himself. *You have a lot to make up for*, he told himself as he slid the tip of his tongue inside her. Harper's taste, the sweet muskiness, was addictive. She was so wet he couldn't imagine it would keep up, but even after an hour the flow of her juices never stopped. With every orgasm, she gushed more and he ardently lapped her up.

"Please," she begged after another orgasm. He felt the tremors throughout her body, how her limbs had become heavy and languid. Sean didn't want to, but he acquiesced. *It's the only way to show you I care.*

He pulled himself up beside her and gently lowered her hands. She continued to shake as she rode the afterglow of her orgasms. With one arm resting heavily across his chest and a leg wrapped around his, he felt the warm stickiness of her center spread over his thigh. "I want you," she said. Her eyes were heavy but her voice was thick with desire. "I need you, all of you," she whispered into his ear. "I just missed you so much…"

With a growl, he rolled on top of her. Harper's legs immediately wrapped around his torso and her heels pulled him against her. He slammed into her and it felt like home.

Harper's eyes were screwed shut as her nails dug into his

back. "Yes," she called out. "Fuck me, thank you. Thank you—"

He buried his head into her neck and breathed in the sugary scent of her. He wasn't going to last long, not this time. "I love you," he breathed into her hair as he released himself into her. She gasped and pulled him deeper inside her, thirsty for every last drop of him.

12

HARPER

*H*e'd taken her body beyond the limits she thought they knew. Harper lost track of how long they'd been in his bed. The cover had long been pushed onto the floor. Sean had taken the length of the black silk flat sheet to create a complicated bind.

"*Hojojutsu*," he'd said as he cinched the material behind her back.

"What?"

"Don't question me," he said sharply. "It's the name of the bind."

The cool silkiness of the sheets were softer than what he'd used before, the rough ropes and police-grade handcuffs. But the intricacy of it, the long ropes of material, made her even more aware of how vulnerable she was.

"Well?" Sean asked. He'd secured the last knot and stood beside the bed. He reached for the full-length mirror next to the bedside table and angled it toward her.

When she saw her reflection, she almost gasped aloud. The contrast of her milky skin against the oil blackness of the sheets, the ties, was almost unnerving. He'd slipped the material around the smallest part of her waist and it framed her breasts. He leaned over and spread her knees wider apart. On her lower half, the black sheet outlined her mound like crotchless underwear. "Do you see how fucking hot you look?" he asked, his voice low against her ear.

She shivered.

"Answer," he commanded.

"Yes, sir," she said.

"And it's all mine," he said. "Say it."

"It's all yours."

"You're all mine."

"I'm all yours," she repeated.

He straightened up before her and went to the closet. When he returned with a basketball, she raised her brows at him. "Sit on this," he instructed. She struggled with her arms bound behind her back, but arched herself up so he could situate the nubby orange ball between her legs.

"Now," he said as he opened the laptop. "Remember this?" He opened a folder and plugged the desktop speakers into the laptop. She heard her own cries of pleasure before anything showed up on the screen. It was deafening, her calls filled the room.

A video of them in the penthouse of the hotel weeks ago appeared on the screen. She blushed and looked away as the Harper on screen greedily dropped to her knees, her hands bound behind her back in handcuffs, and took his cock into her mouth.

"Don't look away," he said brusquely. "You're to watch."

He moved behind her on the bed. She could sense his heat behind her, but he didn't touch her.

"You're going to keep watching," he instructed slowly, "and I'm not going to touch you. Not until you've covered that entire ball with your juices. Do you understand?"

"Yes, sir," she said. On the screen, she watched the Sean of weeks ago stand her up and bend her over the couch. She'd quickly spread her legs and presented her ass to him. However, at the time, she hadn't seen the way he'd gingerly trailed his fingertips along her curves, or the way he'd drunk in her body with so much desire. As the Sean on screen gripped her hips and entered her, he closed his eyes with an expression of so much ecstasy it was almost impossible to keep watching.

From behind her he leaned into her ear. "Look how badly you want me," he whispered. On the screen, she called out his name over and over. He'd picked her up and set her on the couch where she opened her legs as wide as possible. Even on the small screen, and in that dark room, it was clear how wet she was.

Harper watched as the two of them on screen moved in an animalistic rhythm. Every time he drove into her on the screen, she felt it all over again.

"Good girl," he said. She looked down and saw a series of wet trails lick down the basketball. "Watch this," he said. "You're about to squirt all over that twenty-thousand dollar couch."

On the screen, she watched herself squeeze her eyes shut as

she called out, "I'm coming! Oh, fuck, you're making me come."

"Come for me," the Sean on screen demanded. "Right now."

"Oh, fuck!" The stream of her come was evident even with the somewhat grainy footage. The on-screen Sean leaned back to watch. The approval on his face was unmistakable.

"That's right," Sean said behind her. "That's a good girl."

She realized she'd started to grind against the basketball, but she didn't care. On the screen, Sean had reached down to work her clit as she orgasmed, and it forced a new stream of come from her.

"Almost there," he said. She looked down and was shocked by the rivers of wetness that raced down the ball. It was nearly completely soaked.

On the screen, Sean bent down to lick up every last trace of her orgasm. She could nearly feel his tongue on her. "Are you going to come?" he asked. She'd started to bounce on the ball, and didn't give a damn how desperate she looked. She wanted to be treated like an animal, like a bitch.

"Close," she whispered. "I'm close." The unfamiliar roughness of the ball between her legs excited her, but as the Sean on the screen buried his face between her legs and his voice in her ear urged her toward orgasm, it was almost too much to bear.

"Does my sweetheart need some help?" he asked.

"Yes," she urged. "Yes, please." A few more bounces and she'd come all over that ball.

"What's your go word?" he asked.

"Gomorrah," she panted. "Please help me."

He wrapped an arm around her waist to steady her and gripped a length of the taut sheet in his hand. He began to circle her clit with his other hand, commanding an instant orgasm. Harper screamed out in unison with her image on the laptop, coming at the same time as her counterpart from another life.

"You did good," Sean said. He gently pulled the ball from beneath her and held it up so she could see there wasn't even a sliver of dry space. "Taste," he said, and she dutifully licked its rough orange surface.

He set it aside but left the video playing. "Lie back," he instructed.

Harper collapsed onto the bed while shakes from the orgasm still rocked through her. Sean leaned down and kissed one pert nipple, then the other, both pushed out and swollen from the tightness of the bind. "Tell me what you want," he said.

"More," she murmured. She couldn't help the exhaustion in her voice. "I want more."

"Greedy today," he said with a smirk. "How are those ties?"

"Okay..."

"Okay, what?"

"Okay, sir."

"How about we loosen some of them a little?"

He withdrew a six-inch straight blade knife from the tableside drawer and her eyes widened.

"It's alright," he said. "You know your safe words." He loomed over her and traced the tip of the knife around her breasts. Harper stiffened when the pointed end started to outline her areola, but she didn't say a word. "Speak," he said.

"Gomorrah," she said, albeit with reluctance. Still, as the shining cold blade raked across her nipples, there was a fresh gush of wetness between her legs. Sean sensed it and quickly cut away one of the binds.

She held as still as possible as he teased the knife to her other breast, confident in her safety. He wouldn't hurt her, she was sure of it. Just the finest of lines, not even a scratch, lingered where the knife had been. Within a minute, it would disappear entirely.

On her other breast, he was more languid, teased more. There was a moment, just a moment, when she thought he'd press too hard. "Eden," she gasped out. He looked surprised, but moved the knife away from her nipple and lightened the pressure. Sean cut off another part of the complex bind, this one near her oblique muscle.

As he moved the knife downward, she grew even more wet. The danger, the coldness of the blade, all of it had her more ready than she'd ever been. He flicked the blade through the small strip of pubic hair at her mound. "Be still," he cautioned as she opened her legs wider.

He dragged the knife slowly from her groin up her thigh to the inside of her knee. She wanted to wiggle, to ask him to bring it back to her center, but she didn't dare. "Gomorrah," she moaned, and hoped he understood.

Slowly, at a painstaking pace, he moved the blade back to her wetness. As he expertly maneuvered the blade around her outer labia, his other hand pressed her thigh open. Harper felt her clit swell, painful, as he started to explore her inner folds. "You need to trust me," he said, "and hold very, very still."

She gasped as she felt the tip of the blade at her entrance.

"Are you okay?" he asked. "Talk to me."

"I think so. Yeah. Gomorrah," she said.

She felt the blade slip half an inch into her and wanted desperately for him to rub her clit to counteract the fear. "How about now?" he asked.

"I don't ... my clit," she said softly, embarrassed.

"I need you to be really clear with me right now," he said. The blade rested, barely inside her.

"It feels alright, but I need more. Something else ..."

"You can't have anything but this right now, it's too dangerous," he said. "Relax. Try to enjoy this isolated experience."

"Okay," she said. Harper's eyes took in all the details of the ceiling. She counted the lights.

Sean eased the blade just barely deeper inside her. It didn't hurt at all, though the fresh coldness of the blade sent a shock through her. "Eden," she said quickly.

"You're getting so fucking wet," he said. "But I'm going to remove the knife now, slowly. You might come when I do, so try to stay still."

There's no way I'm going to come, she wanted to say. Her body was stiff, unnerved, and wholly aware of the deadly foreign object inside her.

Still, as Sean began to ease the knife out of her, the feeling of complete safety and trust overwhelmed her. She didn't know why tears gathered at her lashes and spilled down her face. "Oh, god!" she called out when there was still half an inch of blade inside her. The orgasm rushed at her, fierce and hard. She didn't expect it, but even as it rocked through her, Sean's words echoed in her head. *Stay still.* She exploded just as he removed the last of the blade. He buried two thick fingers immediately inside her and gave her walls something hot and safe to clench and cling to.

"Are you alright?" he asked softly as the last of the waves subsided. Her cheeks were stained with tears, and she felt forever changed. Whatever had just happened, it bound them together.

He lay down beside her as he easily removed the remaining knots. "Yes," she said. And she meant it, on every level. She burrowed into his neck and inhaled his scent. "I love you," she said. The words just slid out, unbidden.

"Fuck, I love you, too," he said as he pulled her closer. "So much I think I could die."

Her mouth found his as her body gave out, exhausted, to the darkness.

13

SEAN

"What is that?" she asked. The lavender of the morning sunrise pushed insistently against the covered windows.

"Don't ask questions," he said. Sean gestured for her to stand. Harper obliged quickly. He snapped his finger and pointed across his lap. She leaned across him, naked. He felt her heavy breasts as they brushed against his calves and she presented her ass to him. It was already heavily marked with light red and purple bruises for what was going on forty-eight hours of fucking.

He chose a part of her creamy white roundness that was unmarked and spanked her twice, smartly. She grunted, half in pain and half in pleasure. He rubbed comfort into the area. "You know better than that," he said. "Stand up."

Sean peeled off the lip of the black latex tape, thick as duct tape. He assessed her body, though it was unnecessary—he knew every inch of her by heart.

She flinched slightly as he started the complicated process of "dressing" her. "Okay?" he asked.

"Yes," she said. "Gomorrah."

As he wrapped the tape around her curves, he pulled tautly at the most sensitive areas. "This might sting a bit when it's removed," he said as he held the tape over her nipples.

"Yes, sir," she said, and he promptly pressed the tape across her flesh. Her nipples hardened as he smoothed it down with a practiced palm.

It took thirty minutes to dress her properly. The kind of precision it took to highlight every angle, the slope of every hill, was almost meditative. Throughout the process, she didn't speak unless spoken to. She took directions swiftly. Sean framed her triangular valley carefully. When a sheen of wetness appeared and her clit began to swell, he ignored it. Had she whimpered in desire or pressed herself into him, it would have been cause for punishment. Harper learned fast.

Finally, he bound her in a cross-chest box tie. The tips of her pale fingers could barely be seen from the front as they flickered behind her back.

"I'm going to bind your feet," he said. "But you need to get on this first." He went to the closet and pulled out the electronic black saddle. "Do you know what a Sybian is?"

Her eyes grew wide as she took in the monstrosity. Harper shook her head. "No ..."

"No, sir," he corrected.

"No, sir."

"For that indiscretion, I'm not going to spank you," he said. "What I am going to do is start you off without a dildo. Just the vibration. That should be punishment enough for you. I was going to stop you at a three-inch girth," he said as he held up a flesh-colored dildo, six inches long. "But forgetting your manners, I think we'll train you up to five inches of girth today."

She swallowed as he held up the black dildo. Like all the others he'd ordered, it was made specifically for the machine. "Yes, sir," she said.

"Remember your words," he said.

Sean spread a layer of lubricant onto the machine, though he doubted she'd need it. Still, her body had taken a lot in the past couple of days. "I control it with this," he said, as he held up the remote. "Hold still while I bind your feet."

Once she was tied, straddled over the Sybian, it all fit so well it would be nearly impossible for her to dismount on her own. Sean started the Sybian on the lowest vibration, and immediately Harper's eyes rolled back. She started to pant and her nipples pushed against the tape when he kicked it up a notch. His erection pressed against his boxer shorts, but he refused to touch himself.

Her first orgasm came quickly, and Harper ground herself against the machine. "That's good," he said. "Time to start size-training you." He lifted her and moved her a few inches toward the back of the machine while he fitted the smallest dildo onto the Sybian. He'd chosen it to be especially small, less than half his own size, to frustrate and tease her. He lifted her again and eased her onto it. Even that small amount of fullness in Harper made her cry out.

Sean brought her to orgasm a second time with just the slightest bit of edging. With each new dildo, both length and girth increased slightly. She was damp and heavy by the time she reached her fourth orgasm—and where he'd originally thought he'd stop.

He held the black dildo in front of her. By now, she was wet and her muscles were loose from the constant waves of pleasure. "I'm going to unbind you for this," he said. "I need you to have a little more control. Don't take more than you can handle."

"Yes, sir," she said.

He snipped off the tape at her ankles and wrists. Harper leveraged herself over the black dildo that he'd fixed into the Sybian. As she lowered herself onto the tip, knees spread, she let out an animalistic moan.

"Keep going if you can," he said. She lowered halfway onto the dildo. Sean saw her juices had already soaked down to the base.

"Eden," she said cautiously.

"Wait it out if you can," he said. "Just stay there. Think about how full you are. That's a pressure on your G-spot you might not have experienced before."

Her lips had parted perpetually. She was soaked in her own sweat, her own desire. Just the look of her, gorgeous and poised above the machine he controlled her with, was enough to make him almost go over the edge himself.

Harper tried to lower herself farther. "Inferno," she said. She shook her head instinctually. "I can't."

"It's okay," he said. He went to her and helped ease her up. She breathed heavily when the black tip finally appeared. Sean saw the white wet strings of all the orgasms, a thread that trailed from the plastic cock to her middle.

"I'm sorry," she whispered.

"Don't be sorry," he said.

As he laid her on her back, he began to slowly peel away the tape. She did what she could to help and arched her back to provide better access. Harper let out a small cry when he pulled the tape from her nipples, though he did so fast to minimize the sting. After every inch of tape removal, he kissed her tender skin. When he gathered her sore nipples into his mouth, he licked and sucked gently.

When all the tape was finally removed, he nosed to her center. It was easy to see the fruits of his work. She was stretched, though temporarily. He began to lap softly at her clit, and she writhed in pleasure, insatiable. Sean licked up every drop that he'd commanded she release over the past ninety minutes.

Harper lifted her mound closer to his face, and when he obliged with a finger slid deep inside her she let out a sigh of contentment. The smallest sounds of protest came from her when he removed his finger, but she purred in surprise when he moved immediately to her anus and circled her rim.

As she came against his tongue, he wondered if his needs had shifted. *When did the line between degradation and pain get so blurred?* Or perhaps it was her needs that had changed.

Sean raised himself over her when he felt the last surge of her orgasm wane. Harper immediately grasped for his cock, needy and desperate. She called out his name as he buried into her. She nipped at his neck gently, and for a moment he considered punishing her. But it had been hours, and she'd been incredibly obedient. *Let her have her fun,* he thought. The sex was still amazing, but the undercurrent of pure need was new.

"Please come in me," she said. "I need it, please …"

"Are you going to be my good girl, my sweetheart?" he breathed into her ear. "Are you going to clean me up with that mouth afterward?"

"Anything you want," she panted.

"I want you to taste your come all over my cock," he said.

"Yes," she yelled.

"Tell me you're just for me, you're all mine."

"I'm yours," she said. "Please come in me."

Even as he lost himself inside her, spilled his seed into her deepest parts while she writhed in pleasure below him, he couldn't help but worry about everything. They were in unknown waters now, even for him. And he didn't know how long he could stay afloat.

14

HARPER

*H*arper woke with a cough. Water shot from her mouth and raked at her throat. *Why is it so bright?*

As her eyes fought against the warm water, she realized she was in the shower. Her elbow and temple ached, but there was no trace of pink in the water. *I fainted again.*

She didn't know how long she'd been crumpled on the gray wet tiles, but it hadn't been long enough for the water to go cold. A purple shampoo bottle lay beside her. It oozed a rich, bubbling froth.

Harper pushed herself to a seated position and pulled herself onto the wooden shower bench. She hadn't locked the bathroom door and it was still firmly shut. *At least Sean didn't realize,* she thought.

As soon as she turned off the shower, she began to shiver. She wrapped her hair in a towel and slipped into the white Egyptian cotton robe. *Thank god for en-suites,* she thought. It was the only reason he hadn't heard what must have been a terrible crash.

While Harper dried off, she pulled an old favorite white t-shirt from the dresser. It had been one of her staples in the days when she had an average of six go-sees per day. She caught a glimpse of herself in the mirror and delighted at how pronounced her hip bones and ribs were. She could count each rung that flanked her sternum like a ladder.

She paused before the mirror, the shirt caught at her breasts, and pressed her palm into her concave stomach. It was almost unbelievable that there was a life in there. Harper turned to the side to see her figure in profile. That's when it was always the most striking, with no bones splayed wide. The ant-sized waist was still there. Once, a designer had asked her how long she'd waist trained. It was before Harper even knew what that was.

What would it be like to grow something inside of your body? she thought. Obviously, it would include getting fat. She knew that, had read about the relaxin that flooded the body and urged the pelvic bones to spread apart. No matter what, even if she lost the exact amount of weight she put on after the baby, there was no piecing the bones back together.

But wouldn't it be worth it? Worth it to have Sean's baby? Harper's breath caught at the idea of it. This wasn't just a baby, or even just her baby. It was her and Sean's baby. *And it might be the last chance you get.*

The fact that she could even get pregnant was a miracle. She could count how many times she'd had a period in the past ten years. "You have to tell him," she told her reflection. He might be angry, but he'd be rightfully enraged if he found out she'd waited to tell him. *Unless it'll just be a miscarriage*, she thought. That was a stark reality she had to consider. Harper had known countless girls in the industry who miscarried regularly. *Of course, they'd been trying to get pregnant.*

On the other hand, if she miscarried relatively early, she wouldn't have to worry about getting fat. She hadn't even Googled yet how many calories she was supposed to have as a pregnant woman who didn't want to gain excess weight. *Some models did it,* she told herself. *Hell, look at Heidi Klum.* Some of them were back on *Sports Illustrated* covers three months after giving birth.

But Harper knew that came from surgeries she couldn't afford and genes she didn't have. Genetically, she wasn't supposed to be this thin. Every woman in her family had an hourglass shape, but they carried their curves well. She'd had to shed every ounce she could spare to look like this, and it hadn't been easy.

Harper shook her head and pulled down the shirt. She grabbed a pair of jeans so worn-in that they felt like flannel. Pleased that they still fit, that the jeans she'd bought at fifteen still hugged her like a second skin, she took one last admiring look in the mirror. The thigh gap was prominent even in the denim. *Can I really give that up?*

In the living room, she curled up on the couch and opened her laptop. It was full of responses from employers, but she could tell from the subject lines and snippets of opening text that they were all rejections. "Thank you for your application. Unfortunately the position has been filed ..." and "we will keep your resume on file for the next six months ..."

"Fuck you," she said under her breath.

"You're chipper this morning." She jumped at Sean's voice behind her.

"Jesus, you're like a cat," she said.

"More like you're addicted to that thing," he said.

She sighed. "I've been job hunting," she said. "Unsuccessfully."

"You are? What kind of jobs?"

"At this point, anything anywhere they'll take me," she said.

Sean settled onto the couch beside her. "What about modeling?" he asked. "I know the last thing you had fell apart, but I figured—"

"I got fired. Permanently. Basically blacklisted from the industry."

"What? You didn't tell me that."

Her face burned. *I was on my way to tell you that when you got arrested!* "It's complicated," she finally said.

"Try me."

"Okay," she said as she let out a breath. "I'm not thin enough anymore. I'm not young enough. Alright? I'm fat, I'm old, and I was never famous enough for anyone to overlook that."

"That's insane," he said. It was simple, and she could tell that for him it was true.

"Yeah, well. Tell my former bosses that," she said. "Tell the designers. The agents."

"Well … what are you thinking of doing instead? Besides anything anywhere, of course."

"I don't actually know," she said. "If it wasn't for this … arrangement … I don't even know where I'd be right now. I'm running out of money and there are even fewer options. I can't even get a job as a waitress, can you believe that? Actually, never mind. I have zero experience and this town is full of professional waitstaff."

"I have an idea."

"Yeah?" She was doubtful, but at this point desperation overrode just about anything.

"Yeah. There's a bottle of sparkling juice in the fridge. Why don't I set us up two glasses on the patio, and we can talk about it."

Harper felt a half smile on her face. *Sparkling apple juice. At least I don't have to come up with an excuse for not drinking. We can be teetotalers together.* "Okay," she said.

"You go on out to the balcony. I'll be there in a minute."

The warm California sunshine quickly dissipated any chill that lingered in her. Harper slid the Dolce and Gabbana sunglasses onto her nose as she tucked her legs beneath her on the wicker patio furniture. *You can say goodbye to designer sunglasses from here on out,* she thought to herself.

Sean appeared with two crystal flutes and a bottle of sparkling apple juice that sweated in his hands. "Fancy," she said.

"I aim to please," he said. He popped the bottle and the familiar echo made her remember all those nights in clubs after shows. Everything she'd taken for granted.

Sean handed her one of the glasses, one-quarter full of bubbles and froth. "Cheers," he said as he clinked glasses with her. "Look at me," he said suddenly.

"What?" she paused with the delicate flute against her lips.

"It's bad luck not to make eye contact when you say cheers," he said.

"Well, then," she held his gaze. "I'm not in a position to test the waters of luck."

"You and me both," he said. "So, tell me. What kind of jobs have you been drawn toward?"

She hesitated. "Well … I've been thinking about an art gallery."

"Doing what?" he asked. She was surprised that he didn't seem taken aback. Maybe it didn't sound so stupid after all.

"Selling art," she said. "An administrator, they call it."

"Really?"

"Yeah," she said. "I like art, especially contemporary art. And I like connecting people with something they didn't know they needed."

"You are nothing if not a surprise," he said as he took a swallow of the sweet juice.

Harper laughed. "I aim to please," she said with a wink.

"Alright. Well, an art gallery it is. I'll start putting out some feelers. I know a lot of people in the art gallery world here. There's plenty of overlap with the tattoo industry."

"I never thought about that," she said. Although of course it made sense. Art was art, whether it was on a canvas or a body. "But you don't have to do that," she said quickly. "I can figure it out."

"You told me that you love me," Sean said pointedly. "And I told you the same. We're living together, even if the circumstances that brought us here aren't that great. Or orthodox. As far as I'm concerned, we're a team. When you're happy, when your life's a little easier, I feel the same. So, you're right. I don't have to do anything. But I want to."

A warmth spread through her. Harper leaned across the table and pressed her lips to his. She could taste the sweetness of the juice on his tongue as it mingled with her own. *Is this what it's supposed to feel like?* she asked herself as he pulled her onto his lap. *Real love?*

Sean cradled her in his arms and for once she didn't flinch or suck in her stomach when his hand moved across her abdomen. Briefly, she wondered if he knew. If the offer of juice wasn't just because he was sober, but because of what they'd created.

You need to tell him, she reminded herself. But not now. Not when everything was so perfect and it was like every possibility was an option spread out before them.

15

SEAN

The soothing sound of the charcoal on thick paper put Sean into a nearly meditative state. He'd started his first drawing of her. Harper was curled up on the couch. She painted her nails, lost in her own thoughts. She looked up just as he'd finished the rough outline. "Stop," she said as she wrinkled her nose.

"Absolutely not," he said. "You agreed. As long as you don't have to 'pose like one of those French girls' I get to draw you."

She rolled her eyes. "I wasn't being serious," she said.

"Doesn't matter. A deal's a deal."

"You already made a bunch of drawings of me," she said. "They're still covering the walls in your room I believe."

"Those are different," he said. "Those were from memory. Having a live model—and a real model at that—is an elevated experience. Didn't you ever model for a class before?"

"No," she said. Harper blew on her nails, which she'd

lacquered in a cherry red. "Holding still and naked in front of a bunch of people wasn't really my idea of a solid career move."

"You mean you could be naked right now?" he asked with a smile.

"Don't press your luck," she said as she playfully shook the little brush at him.

Harper was perfect in this light. Silhouetted against the window as the sun set behind her. Magic hour, that's what directors called it. Her hair was loosely plaited and fell down her back. She looked like something out of a vintage world, a better world. If he could get it right, it would be the kind of drawing that made everyone who saw it think they'd stumbled into an intimate, secret moment.

"Can I ask you something while you draw?" she asked as she screwed the lid onto the bottle.

"Sure," he said as he replicated the shadows that danced at her collarbone.

"Have you ever thought about the future?"

"That's a loaded question," he said. Briefly, he looked her in the eye. "In what regard?"

"Like, as it applies to you and me."

Sean raised his brow and continued sketching. "A little," he finally admitted. "Honestly, when we first met, I was intoxicated by you. I was more than happy to live in the moment, especially when I wasn't sure you'd have me once you knew ... well, you know."

"What do you see for us, then?" she asked. "Now, I mean. After everything."

Sean paused. "What do you mean?" he asked, though his question was directed at the sketch pad.

"I mean, do you see like a white picket fence? A house, dog, two and a half kids? What?"

"If you're asking me to move to the suburbs, this is a weird way to do it," he said.

"I'm asking how you see things going for us! That's all," she said. There was a touch of impatience in her voice, but Sean had needed to buy that time to think. He knew this conversation was coming, but hadn't expected it to happen so bluntly. However, with the safety of the sketch pad between them, it gave him permission. Permission to be open, honest and let transparency unfold between them. "I don't know," he said. It was true. "I'm not a white picket fence kind of guy," he added. "And, really, I don't think we're a white picket fence type of couple."

"Oh," she said. Harper looked crestfallen, like he'd shattered everything all over again.

"Hey," he said. "Don't get me wrong. I definitely see us together."

"You do?" she asked, hopeful.

"Of course. For the rest of our lives. But ... do *you* really see us as the typical suburban couple?"

"For the rest of our lives?" she repeated. Her eyes were wide.

"Well, yeah," he said. "Don't you? I kind of thought we were on the same page with that. Now, at least."

"I ... I'd hoped so, I guess," she said. "But you have to admit, we haven't really had the most traditional of beginnings."

"Exactly. So why should we have a traditional ending? Is that what you really want—a mortgage, an SUV, some dog with a paisley handkerchief collar? I mean, don't get me wrong. I like dogs, and I like some SUVs. I just never saw myself living out some clichéd American dream. And if I'm honest, I don't see you in that role either. At least not happily."

She blushed. "You're right," she said. "And that's not what I had in mind. The whole suburban dream. It's just the best way I knew how to explain what I was talking about."

"So we don't need to move to the suburbs to be happy?" he asked. "Because I'll be honest, I've never been a fan of Pasadena."

Harper laughed. "This city might have chewed me up good, but I do love it," she said. "So I guess my answer is no. We don't have to move to the suburbs. I don't even want to."

"And the dog?" he asked. "Is that a dealbreaker?"

"I don't particularly have strong feelings about pets one way or the other," she said.

Sean began to fill in the details of the drawing with snippets of glimpses at her. They both knew they danced around the serious subject, those two and a half kids. But it was also a delicious way to tease out the situation.

"I didn't have any pets growing up," he said. "My dad didn't like them, and my mom hated the idea of animal hair, even though we had a daily housekeeper. I always thought it would be kind of cool to have a pet."

"What kind," she asked.

"When I was younger, an English bulldog," he thought. "But now, a pit rescue. You know pitbulls used to be considered nanny dogs by wealthy families? They were so loyal to their families, especially the kids, they'd die for them."

"That's sad," Harper said.

"I don't think so. To be willing to die for your family, for the people you love, I think that's kind of beautiful."

Harper smiled. It radiated the room even in the fading light of the day. "I can see that," she said. "But I thought pitbulls were illegal in California."

"A lot of things are illegal in California," he said. "Sodomy's a crime in California. Doesn't mean it's bad, or that people don't do it anyway."

He smirked when he saw Harper's face go pink. Even after all this time, and after everything they'd done, it was still so easy to make her blush. "Can you keep that color in your face?" he asked. "It's really inspiring."

"Shut up!" she said with a laugh. "Or I'm moving."

"You know, you're right. You really would have made a terrible figure model."

She stuck her tongue out at him. "Thanks."

"Are you going to tell me more about this SUV?" he asked. "Is that your way of saying you don't like my old muscle car? What did Debbie ever do to you?"

"Debbie?"

"That's her name."

"You named your car?"

"I think every guy names his car."

"Why Debbie? Is that like an ex or something?"

"No," he said slowly. "How old do you think I am? Do you know any Debbies in their twenties or thirties? Debbie was one of the most popular names the year the car was made. I picture a Debbie as a video vixen from the early eighties. The kind who would be riding in one of Whitesnake's cars."

"Maybe," she agreed. "But now all the Debbies are middle-aged and middle management."

"Is that what this is all about? Are you trying to get rid of Debbie and replace her with some gas-guzzling SUV?" he teased.

"No," she laughed. "I actually don't care that much about cars. I mean, you've seen mine."

"Your little sedan is cute," he said. "Like you."

"Yeah. And like me it has a few too many miles on it."

"Nothing's sexier than experience," he said. "But Harper? Seriously, whatever you need to be happy, I'll do it. And not because I feel like I should or it's my responsibility or something. It's because I want to."

"Really?" she asked. Harper looked at him, her eyes full of questions.

"Really. You want to get married? Let's get married," he said.

"Don't tease me."

"I'm not. You want to have a huge wedding? Let's do it. Sam specialized in wedding planning before she got pregnant. She'd be thrilled to help you figure it out. A huge cathedral, three hundred people, an eight-tier cake, whatever you want."

"That seems a bit excessive," she said. Still, she'd perked up on the couch. Sean felt a stirring in his jeans as his button-up shirt slipped off one of her shoulders.

"You want to elope?" he asked. "I'm good with that, too. We can book a slot at some little chapel in Las Vegas and let Elvis marry us."

"I have to admit, that's always been kind of a fantasy," she said. Harper began to unbutton the white shirt to reveal the tantalizing creamy flesh beneath. Sean's charcoal flew across the paper.

"You want to have five kids and buy a farmhouse in Vermont? I'm down with that," he said.

"I've always wondered what it would be like to churn my own butter," she said. Harper released the last button and shrugged off the shirt.

"If you want to move to a hut in Tibet, I can do that, too," he said. "I'll go wherever you want to go. Do whatever you want."

Harper stood up and tossed the shirt onto the floor. He could barely make out anything beyond the unbelievable curves of her body's outline. The last of the day's sun hugged her silhouette like a halo.

"What are you doing?" he asked as he swallowed his desire.

"After what you just said, I'm going to fuck you like never before," she purred. "I'm going to fuck you all the way until dawn."

16

HARPER

"Why didn't you tell me?" Sean asked desperately. He was almost impossible to hear over the beeping machines and the stern orders of the doctors and nurses.

Harper was being wheeled down a hallway with long tubes of fluorescent lights in the ceiling. "She's losing a lot of blood," the matronly doctor said. "I don't know if we can save—"

I wanted to tell you. I tried to tell you. She opened her mouth, but the words wouldn't come out. Sean looked down at her, confused and terrified.

"Are you her husband?" one of the nurses asked him.

"Why didn't you tell me?" Sean asked her again.

"Sir! Are you her husband?"

"What? No, I'm—"

"If you're not immediate family, you need to stay in the waiting room."

Harper opened her mouth again to tell them he was wrong. Just confused. He *was* her husband, how could they prove otherwise? "It's not yours." She didn't know where those words came from. It didn't even sound like her voice. But as soon as the words spilled out of her mouth, she could see his heart crack in two.

"It is mine," he said, though his voice was small.

It is yours, of course it's yours. It was too late. She'd already been wheeled through a wide pair of double doors. The last she saw of Sean, he was held firmly by overbearing male nurses or hospital security guards. He'd stared after her, open-mouthed and unbelieving.

This side of the hospital looked decades older. Harper's head lolled to the side and she caught sight of dirt and grime buried into the tile. As she swung her head back to the ceiling to stare at the unforgiving lights, she saw that her swollen belly was uncovered. Four perfectly formed hands pressed against her stomach like they were trying to escape. But they were larger than a baby's should be and awkwardly shaped. The fingers were twice the length of the palm and even through her flesh she could see they came to dagger points.

"What is that?" she asked. "What's inside me—"

"You need to be quiet and stay calm." The doctor leaned over her, a purple face mask obscuring the lower half.

"What's inside me?" Harper yelled as tears ran down her face. They'd pulled her into a cramped room with a single ugly light overhead.

"Strap her down," the doctor barked. Harper felt cold hands at her ankles and wrists. Someone jerked her knees upward and spread her legs apart. The chilled bite of metal on her bare skin shocked her. *Am I naked?*

"What's inside me? Where's Sean?" She tried to look around the room and realized one of the straps had been placed against her neck. All she could do was whip her head side to side.

"Who's Sean?" someone out of her line of vision asked.

"The baby's father—" she tried to explain.

The doctor let out a mean laugh as she picked up a pair of long scissors that looked more like hedge clippers. They seemed dark and rusty. "Sean's not the father," the doctor said. She tsked disapprovingly at Harper. "And those aren't babies."

"What?" Harper strained to see her stomach. Surely those long fingers and talons at the tips hadn't been right.

"We're going to have to remove the parasites," the doctor said. "Unfortunately for you, no anesthesia is possible for such a procedure. Bite down on this if you need to." Somebody shoved a ball gag in her mouth. It was too big and instantly she couldn't breathe. "Hold her legs open," the doctor said. The purple mask leaned over Harper once again, this time from between her legs. "This is going to hurt."

*H*arper woke with a start, her body drenched in sweat. She reached down to inspect her stomach, but it was flat and smooth. "Jesus," she whispered. Sean shifted next to her in bed. She could tell by the light that it was early morning.

Quietly, she slid from bed and padded to the living room. Harper clicked the door shut behind her and grabbed her phone. It was five o'clock in the morning. She tiptoed to her own en-suite and locked the bedroom door. P would kill her for this, but she had to talk to someone.

"Fuck, bitch," P moaned into the phone. "This better be important. Like, you better be dead."

"I'm sorry," she whispered into the phone. "I didn't have anyone else to call."

"Harper?" he asked, suddenly awake. "What is it? Do I need to help move a body? Is camouflage required or will black suffice?"

"I'm pregnant."

"You're *what*?"

Why couldn't you be that succinct with Sean? "I'm pregnant," she repeated. "And I ... I don't know what to do."

"Is it Sean's?"

"Of course it's Sean's! Who else's would it be?"

"I was just checking! God, the pregnancy hormones are already raging, aren't they? So ... what are you doing to do?"

"I ... I think I want to keep it."

"If you want to keep it, you need to stop dieting," he said.

"That was blunt."

"That was real. And you'll probably need some help to get there. Professional help, I mean."

Harper chewed her lip. "I don't know," she said. "Maybe this is all a big mistake. Maybe I'm being a fucking idiot. I'm already jobless. Being jobless and fat at the same time might not be the best idea. Isn't that how most women get dumped?"

"Bitch, shut the hell up," he said. "First of all, there's a big difference between being pregnant and being fat. You need to get your pretty little head around that. You hear me?"

"I hear you," she mumbled. She knew P was right, but her logical side and every other part of her were at strong odds.

"Really?" he said. "Because I don't think you do. Look, baby, I've thought for a long time you needed a little expert intervention. I mean, it wasn't a huge deal when you were twenty years old. A little excessive dieting, maybe even a few bumps at a party to keep your appetite quiet—"

"I never did coke," she said.

"Oh. Maybe that was me. Anyway, what I'm trying to say is back in the day you didn't have any responsibilities. And your body was so young, it could take a little abuse."

"So you're saying I'm old? Being old and pregnant isn't exactly the best combination either."

"Bitch, if you're old then I'm geriatric. And I'm *not* geriatric or old, you got me? All I'm saying is … maybe it's time to start taking a little better care of yourself. And that baby if that's the path you're taking."

"Do you think I'm making a mistake?"

P breathed into the phone. "No," he said. "If you're asking if I think keeping the baby is a mistake, then no. What is a mistake is if you keep abusing your body like that. Baby or no baby."

"Yeah," she said. "I know." Harper's ears perked up. In the

kitchen, she heard Sean start the blender. "Hey, P, I need to go."

"Yeah, just go ahead and wake me up with a bomb like that and take off," he said. "Call me when you figure it out. Or if you need me for anything at all. Okay?"

"Okay, love you," she said.

"Love you, too, whore." Harper made her way to the kitchen.

"Hey," she said with a smile.

"What were you doing in there?" Sean asked.

"Nothing, I just didn't want to wake you."

"I wouldn't have minded," he said as he sipped a green concoction. "I'm going for a shower, if you want to join me."

"Actually, I thought I'd make breakfast," she said.

"Oh." Sean looked surprised. "Alright. I can make it for you, I won't be that long—"

"No, it's okay," she said. "I'll do it."

When she heard the shower turn on, she pulled out a pan and began to whip three eggs into it with a splash of milk. Harper folded in a handful of spinach, but paused at the cheese. An omelet was already fatty enough. Finally, she added a sprinkling of parmesan instead of the shredded pepper jack or cheddar Sean kept in the fridge. *Baby steps*, she reminded herself.

She slid the fluffy omelet onto a plate and halved a few strawberries to go alongside it. Harper managed a few bites of the omelet, and willed herself to eat all of the fruit. The shower turned off, and she quickly spread the breakfast across the plate. It thinned it out, hopefully enough that Sean wouldn't notice.

You're getting fat, the voice inside her head taunted. Her hands roved across her stomach. It was definitely less concave than this morning, the fat from the eggs and cheese already glued to her insides. *Fucking cow. You barely deserve Sean as it is, and then you go and screw it up by getting pregnant? If this baby survives, you're just going to fuck it up like Mom did with you.*

If she just kept restricting like she used to, maybe everything would take care of itself. It would look like a natural miscarriage, and maybe Sean wouldn't even find out. *Why tell him until the third trimester anyway? A lot of people keep pregnancies a secret until then, what with miscarriages being so common in the first trimester ...*

"Stop it," she muttered to herself. Harper piled another bite of omelet onto her fork. It quivered before her lips, a slick glob of yellow. A wave of nausea flooded her, but she forced it into her mouth anyway.

You're so fucking pathetic. She began to retch and spit the partially chewed blob back onto the plate.

Harper rushed to push the remainder of the food down the garbage disposal. She ran the water and turned on the grinder while she rinsed the plate.

Sean appeared just as she flicked off the disposal. "Already done?" he asked.

"I was hungry," she said with a smile. "There's some extra eggs for you if you want it."

"Thanks," he said. "Are you going to the gym?"

"Do you think I should?"

A look of hurt spread across his face. "Not necessarily ... you just usually do this time of day."

"Oh." She was flustered and scurried to cover it up. "I don't know." *The least you can do is skip the gym today.* It was the kind voice, the one she rarely heard. *Give your body a break. Give the baby a break.*

That was some comfort. She watched Sean polish off the eggs in a few fast bites. "You don't need the gym," he said with a smile as he put the pan into the dishwasher. "Come on. I'll give you a workout in bed."

She grinned as he picked her up and carried her into the bedroom.

17

SEAN

*H*arper stretched her limbs on the couch. *She moves like a cat,* he thought as he tore off the charcoal sketch from the pad. Languid and smooth. Once she'd become used to his eye on her, she'd relaxed. Sean set up the stretched canvas on the portable stand and began to mix the acrylics on the same board he'd used for over a decade. It was stained a cocktail of colors, layers deep.

He'd already had every line of her ingrained in his memory, but it was different to allow those lines to flow from his head —from his heart—through his fingers and onto something real. Something tangible. Something he could keep if he loosened his grip and she slipped away.

Now, his fingers full of the muscle memories of her, he could begin the acrylic painting that would keep her. Immortalized.

"What are you doing?" she asked. Harper had tucked into a thick book, long ago given up hope that he'd let go of this project.

"Moving onto acrylic."

"The charcoal's done? Isn't that enough?"

He gave her a half smile. "Charcoal is just a warm-up," he said.

"Can I see?"

"Later. I'd rather you see them both at the same time."

She gave him a faux pout. "Fine," she said.

It took him ten minutes to blend the perfect reds and browns together to capture her hair. It caught fire in certain lights, but burned a slow and deep ember in others. The yellow undertones of her skin, so contrary to the rest of her and cradled below the nearly constant pink glow of her blushes, also took plenty of experimenting.

"Tell me something honestly?" she asked.

"Sure."

"How many other girls have you painted?"

"None. Not like this at least."

"Then how?"

He shrugged. "You know. Live models. I took quite a few classes when I was a kid and a teenager. In college. Occasionally I'd hire my own private models."

"Oh." She worried at her lip.

"Jealous?" he asked.

"No," she said, too quickly.

"Aren't you going to ask what those private models looked like?" he asked.

"No. But if you really want to tell me ..."

He gave a laugh. "There weren't that many. One weighed four hundred pounds. I know because she was quick to tell me. One was a double amputee from a car accident."

"Wait, what?"

"You wanted to know," he said. "I was interested in capturing what we don't usually see in art. What we don't normally consider beautiful. Trust me, it was much more challenging, and enjoyable, than the usual wannabe models that showed up for figure classes. No offense," he said quickly.

"None taken," she sniffed. "I think I worked hard enough to warrant not being envious of a wannabe model. So ... how many times did you paint them? The private models?"

"I met with each of them maybe three to five times each."

"Where are those paintings now? Can I see them?"

"Sure," he said. "But they're in storage, back on the East Coast. Eventually I'll have everything shipped here. They're not the most outstanding in terms of sheer artistic merit, but they're interesting."

Sean's phone vibrated angrily on the glass dining table. "Shit, sorry," he said. "I thought that was on silent." He reached over to switch it off, but paused at the name. Seeing Ashton's name light up his screen shot him back months in the past.

"Who is it?" she asked. Harper sensed the shift in the air.

"I think it's Ashton," he said.

"Seriously?"

"Yeah, hold on." He paused and considered taking the call in the other room. But what was the point? It was the two of them now, Harper and him. She might as well listen. He held up a finger to his mouth and answered the call with speakerphone. "Hello?"

"Sean?" He thought maybe Ashton's voice would have changed since the accident, though that didn't make any logical sense. But it was the same voice he'd known for over a decade. The same voice that egged him on in college, that was cool and soothing on the nights his parents drove him nearly over the edge.

"Hi, hey, Ashton," he said. "How's it going? Sorry, that's kind of a stupid question."

"Yeah. It is," Ashton said. There was an edge in his voice that hadn't been there before. Sean couldn't tell if it was reserved just for him, or maybe it was permanent. "Although I guess I could say I'm better than I was a few weeks ago. Or at least I've been told."

"Ashton ... I'm sorry, man," he said. "For everything, for that night, for taking so long to come and see you." He could feel Harper's eyes on him. When he looked up, she gazed at him with empathy in her eyes.

"You're sorry?" Ashton gave a curt laugh. "Sorry's for bailing on the bar tab. That doesn't really cut it."

"I'm ... I don't know what else to say," Sean said.

"You can start by saying you're not going to cause trouble with the lawsuit. I don't have the time—or the energy—to make this a huge ordeal in court. So I'd appreciate it if you'd just suck it up and do the right thing."

"The right thing? Wait, you're moving forward with the lawsuit?" Sean hadn't heard anything from T, and he knew she wouldn't waste any time if she had news. "Has your attorney talked to mine? Do you—"

"That's a question to ask *your* lawyer," Ashton snapped. "Regardless of what bullshit they discuss though, I can promise you that yes, the lawsuit is moving forward. You're not getting out of this with some kind of deal or plea bargain or any of that crap."

Anger began to simmer in Sean, but he willed it down, swallowed it like an uncomfortable lump in the throat. "And what exactly do you think I'm guilty of?" he asked. "I don't know how much you remember of that night, but you were driving. We were both drinking, but those were your drugs. The blow, the pills—"

"Oh, were they?" Ashton asked. "Can you prove that? The pills were stolen. I know I was the only one with coke in my system, but can you prove you didn't provide it? That you weren't the dealer, not just mine but a shitload of other people's?"

"You know that's not true," Sean said slowly.

"Does a jury know that's not true? How do you think that would look to them? And since I was so messed up, on drugs that it appears you supplied, don't you think you should have taken charge of the situation? Not let me drive? Wouldn't that have been the responsible thing to do?"

"This is bullshit and you know it," Sean said. "What are you getting out of this?"

"Well, for starters, I have a six-figure hospital bill that needs to be paid. But beyond that, my lawyer says I have an equally high amount of pain and suffering he's more than happy to assign a dollar amount to."

"Hospital bills?" Sean asked. "What about your insurance? What—"

"Insurance?" Ashton asked with a laugh. "Yeah, you rich kids take that shit for granted. I was a twenty-something recent college grad and an entry-level job! What kind of insurance did you think I had?"

"So it's about the money," Sean said. *It's always about money.*

"Of course not!" Ashton said. "What is it with you trust fund babies? Always on about the money. It's about the principle, you fucking prick. You got off without a scratch, and I was in a coma for almost six fucking months! Six months I won't get back. And you just got to prance back to your goddamned gilded life like nothing happened—"

"Is that how you think it went?" Sean asked. Harper flinched at the edge in his voice, but he couldn't pull back now. "I was in fucking hell!" he screamed at the phone. "And, in case you weren't informed of this, I spent quite a bit of time since then in jail."

"And you should have! Fuck, Sean, you should be in prison right now! If it weren't for your daddy's money bailing you out—"

"You know what? Fuck you," Sean said. "You want to keep going with the lawsuit, fine. And you want to see what money can really do? Let's just see how your DA does against one of the best attorneys in town."

"You're going to fucking pay—"

Sean reached over and cut off the call before he could hear anything more.

"Are you okay?" Harper asked gently. She moved to get up, but he gestured for her to sit back down.

"I'm fine," he said. "I just need to cool off. You mind if I just keep drawing?"

"I ... I guess," she said. "If that'll help."

"I need to keep my hands busy," he said.

Harper leaned back against the couch and opened her book. He noticed that for several minutes, she didn't turn the page. Her muscles were clenched and her jaw was clamped. Still, the meditative movement of his fingers and hands rocked him back to a soothing state.

What could Ashton really do? Would a judge or jury really buy the whole idea that Sean was some nefarious drug dealer? He shook his head. There was no context for him to gauge either way. But there was also no way Sean would just go ahead and plead guilty to something he hadn't done.

He was already guilty enough, racked with it.

18

HARPER

Harper pressed her lips together as she clicked "book." There was no turning back now—at least not without forfeiting half the thousand-dollar booking fee. She'd spent the past week researching eating disorder rehabilitation options in the Hollywood area. Part of her thought she should go all in *Girl, Interrupted* style, though she wasn't prone to hiding chicken carcasses under her bed.

More realistically, the outpatient options seemed like a better fit. There was no way she could afford inpatient, especially now that her insurance had lapsed, and she wasn't about to let Sean pay for it. Besides, she wasn't that bad. *Am I?*

She'd delved into the first-person accounts and binge-watched *To the Bone* on Netflix three times in the past five days. The feeding tubes, the insane roommates, the banding together to help each other hide the vomiting in the bathroom, it was just all too much. What Harper needed right now was structured support—and Sean. Their situation was already so delicate, and he needed her, too. *What would he think if she just up and left for a stint in rehab?*

Harper sighed. She'd have to tell him now. Fortunately, part of the therapy process at Golden Hills Rehabilitation was working with family and loved ones in group sessions to complement individual therapy. Although she loathed the idea of spilling her worst secrets in front of him, even filtered through a therapist, maybe that's what they needed.

She peeked into the living room and saw him curled over one of his sketch pads. Harper shifted her weight from side to side and practiced her opening line. *Hey, so you know how I'm weird about food?* sounded not serious enough. *Guess what, I'm anorexic. But I'm getting help!* That wouldn't do either.

Harper still didn't know what she'd say as she approached him from behind. Instead, she snaked her arms around his neck and buried her face into his cheek. Sex as a salve wasn't the smartest idea, but it might make for a better introduction to bad news.

Sean went stiff immediately. "What is it?" he asked coldly.

Harper knew that if she pulled her arms away now, it would kickstart a fight. And it would be a fight where she didn't have any leverage. "Nothing," she said meekly. "I just … I wanted to tell you … I've booked myself into an outpatient program. For eating disorders." It was a little easier to tell him like this, not having to see the expression in his eyes. She started at the sketch on the pad. It was her, but she could really only tell from the familiar dress he'd captured. The girl on the paper looked longer and lither than she'd ever be.

"Rehab for an eating disorder," he repeated. It wasn't a question. "Like anorexia?"

"Yeah," she said, embarrassed. "And bulimia, binge eating disorder …" as she let the sentence trail off, she felt a thick veil of shame drape over her.

"And that's what you wanted to tell me? Anything else?" he asked coldly.

She felt a small piece of her die inside, just crumple up and fall away. *This is exactly why you shouldn't tell him,* she chided herself. *Now what are you going to do?* "No, nothing," she said meekly. Slowly, she unwound her arms and retreated back to her room. There was no telling when he'd be in one of his moods. And once he was in them, she couldn't gauge when he'd come out. It could be minutes, hours, or a couple of days.

Harper clicked the door quietly behind her and flopped onto her bed. As she opened her laptop, she clicked through the saved movies on Netflix. She loaded the *Thin* documentary as she prepared to lick her wounds.

Sean burst through the door right as the opening credits started. "Jesus," she said and snapped the laptop shut. For a few seconds the music still played from the speakers.

He stood in the doorway, nearly took up all the space. For a moment, he wavered, uncertain. "If you need to get help, you should," he said finally. "I'm ... I'm here for you. I'm sorry, I'm not very good at this."

All the years of restriction, of fat pinching and measuring bubbled up inside her and began to pour down her cheeks. She was racked by decades of self-hatred and there was no stopping the ugly sobs once they started. Harper reached for words that were buried deep inside her, not even knowing what they were. But the sheer pressure of keeping it all down kept them from coming out.

Sean came to her, sat on the bed and held her close. She cried into his shoulder. "No," she finally choked out. "You're full of crap," she said. "I'm a fucking mess, I know it." Once the words started, they wouldn't stop. "You know what's going to happen, don't you? I'm going to get fat. Even without the feeding tubes and everything, they make you fat in those places."

He stroked her back, firm yet soft. "You're not fat now, and you're not going to be fat if you get help. You'll get healthy."

"Healthy's just a nice way of saying fat," she said. Harper pushed her closed eyes into his shirt and let it sop up the saltwater. "And all this body positivity shit that's going around now. Talking about 'vanity sizing' and that fucking shit. People think fat is good now!"

"First of all, a person can't be fat anyway," he said. "Fat's a necessary part of the body. You can have fat, and it can shrink or expand, but you can't be fat. Second of all, if you're passing out and making yourself throw up—are you making yourself throw up?"

She couldn't bring herself to admit that, but nodded guiltily into his shoulder.

He sighed. "Harper. That's a sign that you're hurting your body. Maybe permanently. I don't know that much about all this, but I'll learn. But I have heard about what bulimia can do. The ruining of the throat, your teeth ..."

"My teeth are fine," she said defensively. It was only partially true.

The last time she'd been at the dentist, months ago, he'd finished the exam and looked at her sternly. "Are you purging?" he'd asked. She was shocked into silence. Harper had never been asked so bluntly before.

"Just sometimes," she said. "I'm a model, so—"

"You need to stop. The acid is wearing away the enamel on your teeth. And I can tell from the severity it's not just sometimes."

She'd kept her eyes on her lap. "Isn't there something you can do—"

"*I'm* doing everything I can," he said. "This is up to you. If you keep it up, though, you'll be having most of your teeth extracted and dental implants before you're forty."

Forty had sounded so old, so far away. There was no way she'd be a model at forty. What was the point in worrying about it?

"Harper." Sean's voice brought her back to the present. "I'm proud of you for getting help. I'll support you in it whatever way I can."

She started to pick at a cuticle as he cradled her in his lap. "Eating like this ... it's the only thing that keeps me thin," she said. "I'm not naturally thin like a lot of the models. Nobody in my family is super thin. And I'm getting older. My metabolism is fucked to hell anyway. I don't want to get fat ..."

"You're not going to get fat!" he said. "And, besides, it wouldn't matter to me if you did."

"Don't lie," she said. "I know that's part of why you like me. You really think you would have been into me if I didn't look like I do? Or did, I should say, when we met?"

"I'm not lying," he said. "And of course I thought you were hot when we met. I still do—more so, though, because I see you. All the way through, to the core. You think those eighty-year-old couples would find each other hot if they met then? It's because they love each other. I love you, and to me you'll always be beautiful. You'll always look like you did the day we met. That's just how it works. You captured my heart, and what you look like is no longer part of the equation."

"Really?" She raised her head and searched his eyes, but could find nothing of trickery in them.

"Yes. Really," he said.

She raised her mouth to his. He tasted of morning tea and an undercurrent of sweetness. As his hands moved from her waist to her breasts, she raised her arms and allowed him to remove her shirt. But when he went to flip her onto her back, she resisted.

Harper pushed his chest and straddled him as he leaned back on her pile of pillows. She could feel the hardness beneath his jeans press into the thin material of her silk panties. His hands reached beneath her short jersey skirt and he squeezed her ass as she released his cock from the denim.

"Hey, hey," he said. "Slow down."

"No," she said, shocked when he listened. Desperate to have him inside her, Harper reached between her legs and pushed the soaked material to the side. She groaned as she directed him into her.

As she began to ride him, her palms flat against his chest, she knew she should tell him about the pregnancy. *But not yet*, she thought. She'd done enough confessing for one day.

19

SEAN

Sean pulled into the small parking lot nestled into a side street of Hollywood Boulevard he'd never noticed before. "I read that celebrities come here," he said as they looked at the nondescript building.

Harper let out a laugh. "I don't know if that's a good thing or a bad thing."

He looked at her. "You'll do great," he said.

Sean opened the glass doors for her and they were greeted with what looked like a combination of a waiting room and the reception area to an upscale retirement home.

"Can I help you?" He couldn't help but check the size of the woman who worked at the front desk. Sean didn't know if most people who worked in eating disorder facilities were in treatment, but she looked healthy. Like she worked out, but not excessively. However, he could see how in a place like Los Angeles, she'd be told she had a pretty face, but should lose at least twenty pounds.

"I have an appointment. Harper—"

"Yes, I have you," the woman said with a chirp. She glanced around at the people who lingered nearby. "We prioritize discretion here," she said kindly. "So don't worry about sharing your surname or any personal details in common areas."

"Oh. Thanks." Harper looked at him strangely.

"I told you they treat celebrities here," he said.

"And are you her husband?" the woman asked.

"Uh, no."

"He's my boyfriend," Harper said. It was the first time she'd said it since they'd gotten back together, and it was so natural. Boyfriend. Like everything that had happened between them was perfectly necessary.

"I'm sorry, but only family members are allowed on the first day. Dr. Horst can arrange for future joint sessions if you'd like."

"Oh. Okay," Harper said. She gave him an apologetic look.

"It's okay," he said, though his heart sank. He'd spent the past three days amping himself up for this appointment. Sean had even researched what kind of support he'd be expected to survive on her road to management. "I'll either go back home or find something around here to do. When will she be ready?" he asked.

"At least three hours."

He watched as Harper flew through the paperwork and ticked off YES to a myriad of responses. At first, she angled the papers away from him. By the third page, she seemed to be checking the affirmative box for just about everything. *Do you think your eating habits negatively impact your social life? Do you sometimes eat in secret? Do you sometimes eat to the point of pain, well beyond being full? Have you ever self-induced vomiting? Do you often choose the wrong, larger size, of clothes when shopping?*

Sean wanted to ask her about it. *Is this really what your life is like on a daily basis?* But he knew just letting him see the responses was a huge step for her.

He looked around the waiting room and played a game. Patient or visitor? Sometimes it was obvious, but for the most part it wasn't. There were men and women, all ages and sizes. Some clearly had money, or at least spent it, while others looked like they could have been waiting for the city bus.

The squeak of rubber shoes on the floors and the overtly plastic greenery were eerily familiar. So was the scent of industrial cleaner. All rehabilitation centers were the same at the core. He remembered his own admission, even through the haze of the worn-off alcohol. How the receptionist offered up the same, tight, toothless smile. How the cheap waiting room furniture looked more tired than any of the people who sunk into it, though the style suggested it was new.

Most of all, he remembered how he felt under the glare of those bright lights—so raw, like he was on display for the world to see. His first day had been raw and painful. There had been a thread of fear that ran through him like he'd never known before. Scared, not knowing what to expect, his own admission had been marinated in moments of sheer terror. But when he glanced at Harper's face, she seemed calm and collected. Maybe that was the big difference. She'd chosen to come here, had probably torn it apart in her head a thousand times. Sean had been dragged. There had to be a huge difference between signing up for swimming lessons and when someone else pushed you into the deep end.

It hadn't just been the drying out that had him on edge during his own rehab. It was the demand that he face his feelings instead of numbing them. How he'd been commanded to reach into the ugliest parts of himself and turn the pieces over and over.

"Well. I guess this is it." Harper's voice brought him out of his thoughts.

"You ready?" he asked as he stood up with her.

"As ready as I'm going to be," she said with a shrug.

A nurse was paged to escort her to her first meeting. Sean watched her thin figure retreat until it disappeared around a corner.

"She'll give you a call when she's ready," the receptionist said. "You're welcome to wait here. We have a small café down that way."

"No," he said, almost too quickly. "I'll just wait for her to call." He didn't want to tell the receptionist that he couldn't stand to sit there any longer. That the walls crept closer with every minute.

As soon as he slid into the driver's seat, he whipped out the phone and called Joon-ki. "Hey! Good to hear from you. Everything okay?" Joon-ki asked.

"Everything's okay with me, yeah," he said. "I just dropped Harper off at rehab."

"What?" Joon-ki's voice changed. "Sean, you didn't tell me

she was an addict. You know how dangerous it can be for you—"

"Rehab for anorexia," he corrected quickly.

"Oh. That's ... I'm sorry. Is everything okay?"

"I guess it's as good as it can be. It's outpatient, at least for now. You working?"

"Just finishing up," Joon-ki said.

"Must be nice, being done with work on a Thursday at ten in the morning."

"Yeah, the great joys of being a systems integration specialist. That's why we have grads lining up around the block to take over our jobs."

"I think you're spoiled. You've been setting your own hours and working from home too long."

"Maybe," Joon-ki admitted. "Did you want to meet? Go to a meeting? How long do you have?"

He paused. A meeting would help pass the time, maybe settle his nerves. "Yeah, sounds good," he said as he checked the time. "Meeting's not for an hour. If you want to grab coffee before, it's my treat."

"Sure, are you in Hollywood? Just give me fifteen minutes."

"Yeah, let's do the one oh one."

Sean waited for Joon-ki in the kitschy diner with a thick white mug of the drip of the day cradled in his hands.

"Hi," Joon-ki said as he slid his narrow frame into the vinyl booth. "You look on edge."

"I feel even worse," Sean said.

"Why's that?" Joon-ki smiled up to the waitress and ordered his usual, with an extra shot in the dark.

"I feel like I failed her," he said. He'd had one quarter of an hour to think about his first line, and that was the best he'd come up with.

"An eating disorder is a mental disorder," Joon-ki said gently. "One of the deadliest and most underdiagnosed. For all you know, your support partially helped her find the strength to seek out help. And I'm guessing that she's suffered from anorexia for several years. How could you have failed her?"

"I didn't see," Sean said quietly. "She was right. She was ... so scared that I'd up and leave her because she wasn't going to be a model anymore. She's terrified she'll get fat. And maybe she's right."

Joon-ki raised a brow at him, but didn't say anything. He'd never judge.

"Not that I'd leave her. Or that she'll get fat, not that that matters," Sean said quickly. "But maybe she's right that I fell for her because of how she looks."

"Sean, that's natural! There's nothing wrong with being attracted to the person you're with. Or for that being the driving factor when you first meet. You don't have to be a martyr, and go around seeking out people you're intentionally unattracted to just to prove something."

He sighed. "I know, but maybe I did something that made her feel like her looks are all that mattered."

"I can promise you that it was society that did that. And the industry she's been in for however many years now. Sean," Joon-ki said as he reached across the table and gently touched his forearm. "I don't mean for this to sound rude, but don't you think it's a little egotistical to think that you drove a girl to an eating disorder after just a few weeks?"

He could feel his ears burn. "Well, when you put it like that …"

"It's really easy for us to blame ourselves when somebody we love struggles with something like this. Will you be going to therapy with her?"

"I think so. At least sometimes."

"Then whatever issues may have impacted her disorder will be addressed and hashed out there, with a professional mediating. Just save these fears and feelings for those sessions. Not that you can't talk to me, of course. I'm glad that you trust me. I just want to make sure you bring this up in therapy, too."

"Yeah," Sean said as he nodded. "I will."

"Just remember that it's not about how you feel. Her process is about how she feels. She'll be fragile right now, so just protect her to the best of your ability."

"Thanks for the reality check," Sean said. "I needed that."

"Should we head to the meeting?" Joon-ki asked as he finished the coffee to the dregs.

"Let's do it." They stood up and Joon-ki clapped him on the shoulder as they headed to the church across the street.

20

HARPER

Harper put down the toilet lid and sank onto the hard plastic seat. Outside, her escort, a girl whose name she'd already forgotten, waited patiently by the sinks. Harper could see her shoes with their thick soles, but nothing else. The girl listened for the sounds of gagging.

Day three of rehabilitation and it ate away at her. She hadn't expected it to be so hard. Of course she knew it wouldn't be easy, but this was like being drawn and quartered. For the past six hours in group, she'd been slammed with everyone's stories. She'd expected that—but what she hadn't expected was to see so much of herself reflected in them.

There was Billy the ballet dancer, who everyone quickly dubbed Billy Elliott. Today, he talked about the time he'd restricted himself so severely for three days before a performance that when it came down to it he couldn't even dance. He'd wanted to look flawless in his skintight, beige costume and hadn't even brushed his teeth for seventy-two hours because he thought a drop of water might make its way down his throat. The lack of food and water had punched up his insomnia. When he'd arrived at the performance, he hadn't slept in thirty-five hours and had passed out before he could even get his costume on.

"That was my last chance, that's what the director said." He said it so matter-of-factly, like everyone got kicked out of one of the best dance companies in the world. Billy didn't look older than nineteen, and his life was already over. *And here I am complaining about not modeling for another decade.*

There was the forty-three-year-old mother of two who traced her anorexia to the year her second daughter was born. "It started out, you know, normal. I just wanted to lose the baby weight," she said with a shrug. "I was thirty-six at the time and certainly didn't fit the mold of what an anorexic should look like."

"Anoretic," one of the thinnest girls replied. Nobody liked that girl, and it wasn't just that she tried to play therapist. Harper had instantly sized herself up against everyone in the room and knew this girl's thighs were at least half her size.

"It doesn't matter," the group leader, a doctor decorated with three degrees, said. "Please continue."

The mother sighed. "I mean look at me!" she said. "I was closer to forty than thirty, half-black, not exactly rich … who would have thought I'd get an eating disorder? I mean, I know anyone can have an eating disorder," she corrected herself quickly. "But, you know, I just didn't think it would happen to me. I just … it started with a diet. With working out more. I hadn't been to a gym in like four years. And when I got to my first goal weight, why not set it even lower? I was getting attention from men who weren't my husband for the first time since college. All these women were telling me how great I was looking … and then that I was too thin. To eat a cheeseburger and all that. And that's what really felt good. You know? Women, they stop complimenting you when you turn into a threat."

That hit home for Harper. It was true. Women were quick to pile on the compliments to fat women. *Your tits are amazing! You have such a pretty face.* But when you were really hot? They got nasty. It was how you could tell you looked good.

"Harper?" the group lead asked as she turned to her. "Is there anything you'd like to share today?"

"Um ... no. If that's okay," she said.

"Of course. It's a good idea to listen during your first week. Observation is a great way to get your feet wet."

"Harper? Are you okay?" The escort's voice sounded like a boom in the otherwise unoccupied bathroom.

"Uh, yeah!" Harper said. "One minute." She thought about flushing the toilet, but didn't bother. The girl knew she hadn't done anything in there anyway.

When she emerged, she was greeted with a small but kind smile. "If you ever just need to get away while you're here, decompress, you can always go into one of the meditation rooms," the girl said. "Trust me, they're a lot more comfortable than the bathroom."

"Thanks," Harper said. She used the last of her day's strength to offer up her own smile.

She made her way into the bright sunlight and was thankful for the familiar scent of her car. For the first two days, Sean had driven her, but she felt guilty. Why should he spend his day chauffeuring her around? Outpatient was supposed to help keep life as normal as possible.

Exhaustion spread through her, all the way to the marrow, on the short drive home.

"How was it?" Sean asked when she walked inside. He had his feet up on the coffee table and a sketch pad in his lap.

"Tiring," she said. "It's going to be an early night for me."

"Sounds good to me," he said. "You want some tea?"

"No, thanks," she said. "I think I'm just gonna lie down for awhile."

"Okay. Let me know if you need anything. I'll be out here with my charcoal."

She ran her fingers through his thick dark hair as she walked to her bedroom. Harper was surprised at how unobtrusive he was. How he could balance on the precipice between caring and respectful. She'd somewhat expected him to go all in on therapy, but since the first day he'd kept a watchful distance. It was nice to be able to come home and not relive the past however many hours of therapy she'd endured.

As soon as she flopped on her bed, she knew she wouldn't be able to sleep. Instead, the stories from group just kept knocking around in her head. There was another model in the group, though her career had largely been in London. She'd moved to her aunt's house in Hollywood to get away from the scene that had nurtured her bulimia and anorexia.

She was pretty, fair, and still a teenager—the epitome of the kind of girl who starved herself. "I don't really know when it started," she said with a shrug. "I ... like I remember my mum talking about liquid diets when I was around ten. I asked her if I could do it, too, and she said alright. I don't think I really wanted to lose weight then, you know? It just sounded fun, like a challenge. And very adult."

"Can you recall the first time you did take action toward restricting to alter your body?" the therapist said.

"Not really," the girl said. "But I remember the first time I was really aware of what fat was. My mum, I think she always talked about how you could tell if a girl was prone to fat by her upper arms. I think I was in … second grade, I think you call it here. Like seven years old. I'd never thought of that before," she said with another shrug. "But I started looking at other girls in class. And at myself. I practiced holding my arm away from me in the mirror so it wouldn't get all pressed and fatter looking. You know? And then … we had these kind of lavish school lunches. It was a private school, kind of posh. But very English, with lots of meats and fat and everything. I started only eating the veggies, fruits and bread. Then eventually just a couple bits of the vegetables."

"And how did your classmates react to this? Your teachers?"

"They didn't," she said simply. "I mean, I got good at making up excuses to 'eat' in various study places or whatever. I … I never had that many friends. So it's not like it was hard to keep it a secret."

Harper knew how that felt. She couldn't recall a single good friend from her childhood. "Models don't need friends," her mom always said. "Why bother? You'll be flying off to shoots when they're talking about what to wear to homecoming."

A lot of the girls in the group drove away everyone around them—or at least everyone who could possibly help them. Instead, they held tight to the ones who encouraged their restriction. Almost every time, if there was another person involved, it was their mother. Although sometimes it was a boyfriend. One who called them fat and worthless, so they tried to buy his approval with their life.

She needed something to busy her mind. *I don't want to be like them,* she thought. She grabbed *The Goldfinch* by Donna Tartt from the shelf. It had collected dust for months. If she could escape into the life of an orphaned boy enthralled in the art world, maybe she could stop thinking about fat, calories, and the skeletons that talked around her all afternoon.

Sean looked up when she shuffled into the living room and sat across from him, but he didn't speak. He went back to drawing.

Harper cracked open the book and breathed in its scent. It was nice, this cozy silence. She realized she'd never had that before, not with anyone in her life. She'd always been in the midst of a cacophony of noise, and had assumed that it was natural. *What will it be like, letting my own thoughts, my own voice, emerge?*

21

SEAN

His eyes had started to grow tired. *Looking for commercial real estate in Los Angeles is the job of a broker*, he thought to himself. Still, when Connor had asked him to scout some spaces for the company, he'd been quick to agree. He needed to prove himself to his brother, to show that he could be an important part of the startup.

Plus, if he could find the perfect space, it might encourage Connor and Sam to move to the West Coast faster. Sean had started to think that maybe they'd just set up shop on the East Coast. Their baby wasn't even here yet and they were already getting into nesting mode. *What if the idea of moving seemed like too much once the baby was born?* Sean didn't know if he even had a job in the company if they stayed back east—or if he'd be able to move.

Harper had started to adjust to the almost-daily outpatient visits, and he wasn't going to ask her to switch facilities. He certainly wouldn't put the stress of moving on her. Besides, who knew if she'd even want to move if he asked?

The door slammed shut and Sean looked up with a start. "Hey," he said as he glanced at the time. "I didn't realize how late it was. How was it today?"

She shook her head, but he knew that look. Harper tried valiantly to hold it all together. "How'd it go?" she repeated. "It's fucking day five of rehab and ... never mind."

He wanted to push, to prod, but he knew better. In between the constant hunt for real estate, he'd seasoned his day with researching eating disorders. He didn't know what she was upset about, but knew that there would be a lot of inky emotions erupting from her for awhile. There was no telling what they'd talked about today, and their joint sessions hadn't even been scheduled yet.

Harper opened her mouth to say something, but slammed it shut again. Instead, she went to the sink and filled a glass with water. He felt her eyes as they stole glances in his direction, but he had to wait it out. *Let her come to you*, he told himself. *She'll talk when she's ready.*

But she finished the glass of water and lingered by the sink.

"What?" he finally asked as he looked her in the eye.

She bit her lip and shook her head. Sean stood up and went to her, but she busied herself with excessively rinsing the glass.

"You can talk to me. If you want," he said gently as he rubbed her arm.

"You'd better sit back down," she said.

"Is this ... Harper, is everything okay?"

"You'd better sit down," she repeated.

He sucked in his breath as they both perched precariously on the edge of the sofa. Sean searched her face for clues, but found nothing. "Sean, I love you. You know that--"

"Are you breaking up with me?" he asked. It sounded like a breakup speech, and his heart sank. *Less than a week in rehab and she'd already identified the problem,* he thought to himself.

"No!" she said. "Don't be weird. Just ... let me get this out."

"Okay," he said, though a big part of him didn't want to hear whatever speech she'd prepared.

"I thought ... I thought we were being safe. But ..." she trailed off and stared at the exposed brick wall. Tears started to stream down her face, but they were silent.

"Safe?" he asked with a shake of his head. "Safe ... hold on. Are you ... are you pregnant?"

She nodded, and the floodgates opened. With an open-mouthed sob, it all poured out.

"Are you sure?" he asked, though he knew it was a stupid question. Not only was she obviously sure, but so was he. He'd never considered it before and had assumed she was on birth control. A baby was so far out of reach for what he'd imagined his life to hold, it had never even crossed into the equation. *But a baby?* The idea of it felt right. Especially with her.

"Say something," she said between sobs.

"I ... I never wanted kids. If I'm being honest," he said. Her cries cracked the silence in the room. "But, hey!" he said as he moved across the couch to close the space between them. "Sorry, I'm bad at this. I didn't mean it like that. I mean it's ... exciting. Don't you think?"

"Exciting?" she asked. Harper had pulled the long sleeves down over her hands and pressed a cotton-encased fist against her cheeks to dry them.

"Well, yeah! I was serious when I said it was up to you with what our lives would be. That is, if you want to keep it. That's why you're telling me, right?"

"I don't ... I don't know," she said.

"Of course you know."

"You're right," she said, and a slip of a smile appeared on her face. "I do know. I want to keep it. God, I haven't said that out loud yet."

"It's, you know, a little earlier than I would have expected. If I'd been expecting it at all. But what can you do? We've never been the most conventional couple." He wrapped his arms around her and breathed in the scent of her hair as she nuzzled into his chest. A fresh wave of sobs began to rock through her. "Hey," he said softly. "What is it? Isn't this supposed to be a happy moment?"

"It is," she said with a half-laugh, half-cry. "It's just ... the baby is why I'm in rehab."

"Oh," he said. "That makes sense. How long have you—never mind. It doesn't matter."

"We were talking about the importance of truth in group today," she said. Harper pulled herself up and let him wipe away the tears. "Not just being truthful to ourselves, but to everyone important in our lives. And I just needed to tell you. You know?" she asked.

"I know."

"I've been trying for a couple of weeks now to figure out the right way to say it, and I just couldn't come up with anything. There's no great way to say it, especially when you don't know how it will be received."

"You didn't think I'd be happy?" he asked, wholly amazed.

"I didn't know," she said with a shake of her head. "I didn't even know if I was happy about it for a long time. I … you know, I worried. First about getting fat, even though logically I know that's stupid. But also about the baby. Like, how could I give a baby proper nourishment when I can't even do that for myself? I didn't have my period for so long. So many models have miscarriages, so there was that."

"You'll be a great mom," he said. "You already are. Look at you. Prioritizing your health. You're doing everything right."

"I am," she said. He couldn't tell if it was a question or a statement, but either way he saw the certainty settle into her face.

Sean kissed her forehead. "I'll be the first to say maybe the timing isn't perfect. It's not convenient. But when has anything about our relationship been perfect or convenient?"

She looked up at him. "So you're not mad?" she asked. "Honestly. Just tell me if you are, because I don't think I'll be able to get together the courage or strength to have this conversation all over again."

"Of course I'm not mad," he said. "I'm excited. And terrified, and worried, and a shitload of other emotions I can't even name right now." It was strange but it felt right to so blatantly tell her the emotions that pulsed through him.

"You're terrified?" she asked with a small laugh. "I'm so scared sometimes I can't even move. Seriously, every little decision I make now, I'm like, is this what the baby wants?

I've been trying to figure out the best prenatal vitamins to take for two weeks."

"You're not taking any?"

"I am," she said. "I finally just picked the ones with the best and most reviews on Amazon. They're organic. I mean, aren't most vitamins? I don't know."

"Have you seen a doctor?"

"Not really," she said. "I mean, there are doctors at rehab, so I guess so. I found out in the hospital. With the blood tests they were running for other things."

"This is crazy," he said with a small laugh. "A good crazy, but still. I have to say, when you walked into that tattoo shop and asked for a tramp stamp, this isn't where I thought we'd be a few months later."

"Hey!" she said with a laugh. "I thought you said it wasn't a tramp stamp."

"I never said that, sweetheart," he corrected her. "I said there's nothing wrong with tramp stamps."

"Oh, god," she said. "What are we going to do?"

"Most people, since the beginning of time, have had a baby," he said. "If they can figure it out, we certainly can."

"You sound pretty confident about that," she said.

"I am. But there's one thing I know for sure."

"What's that?"

"We're going to make a kind, intelligent, gorgeous baby. How can we not since it'll be half you?"

She smiled up at him. "Like I said. Pretty confident."

"And pretty scary."

"Yeah. That, too. But you're right. If billions of people can do it, we can probably swing it."

"You know what this means, right?"

"What?"

"You're totally going to steal Sam and Connor's thunder."

She groaned. "Don't remind me."

"I'm just teasing. They'll be thrilled. And Sam is going to throw you one hell of a baby shower."

"I don't even want to think about that right now. God, I'm so tired."

"Tired from therapy or the baby?"

"Probably both," she said with a groan. "But telling you helps alleviate some serious weight."

22

HARPER

*H*arper stared at the ceiling while Sean slept peacefully beside her. She ran her hand across her stomach, but felt nothing save for the shallow echo of her own heartbeat. Her back ached. The bed was nearly brand new. It had to be one of the first of many pains to come.

She slid out of bed quietly and pulled a stretchy pair of pajama bottoms on. *Are these tighter than they used to be?* she wondered. A trick she'd learned in group was to look at numbers that weren't on the scale when she began to wonder if her body dysmorphia disorder was acting up. Vanity sizing or not, there was no way a so-called "fat person" could wear a size two or an extra small. The pajamas might be stretchy, but they were still a size zero.

Harper tiptoed into the living room and eased the door shut behind her. As soon as she sat down on the couch and opened her laptop, the pain that gnawed into her back turned into a full-blown ache. It was worse than the period cramps that haunted her in middle school—and those were bad enough that after a few months of taking days off school, she was given prescription painkillers. At fifteen, her mother had taken her in for a Mirena IUD to stop the periods and pain altogether. It hurt so badly going in that, at twenty when it was time to replace it, she'd gone back to the pill. Fortunately, by then the worst of the menstrual pains seemed to be behind her.

She sucked in her breath with a hiss as the pain seemed to snake from her back to her stomach. Harper looked toward the closed bedroom door, but she didn't want to wake Sean. She was still in her first trimester and wasn't even showing. How weak would she look if she woke him up to complain about pregnancy pains this early on?

Instead, she picked up her phone and made her way to the balcony, though she had to pause every few steps to hold her throbbing stomach. She called P, but when he answered she could barely hear him. The drum of house music blasted through the phone.

"Where are you?" he yelled in his semidrunk voice. "You should be here, this place is fire."

"I think something's wrong," she said.

"What? I can't hear you."

"Go somewhere quiet!"

"Slow your roll, ho, I'm going." Suddenly, the music came to a halt and she heard a door slam on the other end. "Now, what?"

"P, I think something's really wrong."

"What happened? What do you mean?"

"My back, and now my stomach. It hurts really bad. I thought it was just cramps, but it won't stop."

"It's one in the morning. Where's Sean?"

"Here. Asleep."

"And you didn't wake him up?" There was no trace of revelry left in P's voice.

"I didn't want to seem like a pussy," she admitted. "Like, I'm barely pregnant and I wake him up in the middle of the night because my stomach hurts?"

"If it hurts, it hurts," he said. "I got you. You want me to come right now?"

Harper looked into the distance. Part of the Hollywood sign was visible and lit turquoise pools spotted the dark landscape.

"Harper?"

"Yeah," she said. "I'm sorry, but I do."

"Don't be sorry," he said. "I'm coming now. I'm in the valley, though, so—"

"What are you doing in the valley?"

"It's a Tuesday night. If you want to find the good parties, you have to be willing to travel to different zip codes."

A fresh bolt of pain shot through her. "Just hurry," she said.

"I'm getting in the car now. But seriously? You need to wake Sean up and tell him. He'll find out once I get there anyway."

"No," she said. "I'll … I'll leave him a note. He sleeps like the dead anyway."

"Leave him a note? Hold on, what are we doing?"

She gave a short cry. The pain came in waves, and at the peaks it was blinding. "I think I need to go to the ER."

"I'm coming."

Harper made her way back inside and dug through the foyer table for a pad of paper and pen. *S, don't freak out. P took me to the hospital. It's probably nothing, but will let you know when I know anything. Love, H.* Don't freak out. Yeah, that's the perfect way to start a note. *He'll never read it,* she thought. He hadn't set the alarm, and chances were he wouldn't even wake up for another nine hours. She'd be back and in bed with him by then.

She caught a glimpse of herself in the mirror and made a face. Her hair was a mess and the cracked graphic tank top clashed with her pajama pants. But the idea of changing clothes was too much. *Besides, who looks good in the ER in the middle of the night?*

Harper slid on her gym shoes and grabbed her purse just as P texted her. *Downstairs.*

"What are you wearing?" she asked as he jumped out of the Explorer and helped her into the passenger seat.

"I like to call it club leather meets wayward dominatrix with a heart of gold. Nailed it?" he asked.

She eyed him in his studded leather chaps with the two-foot fringe and snug leather vest. "The leather pageboy hat really ties it all together," she said.

"Oh, good! I thought that might be too much," he said as they pulled away from the building. "So, tell me more. What's wrong, exactly?"

"It's just really intense pain. Mostly in my abdomen now. It comes in spurts, though."

"Maybe it's gas," he said.

"Thanks."

"What! Pregnant women are gassy. At least my sister was. So, what's the story when we get there? Am I supposed to be your black, fabulous sugar daddy turned baby daddy or what?"

"Um, if they ask, which I don't think they will, let's just go with the truth."

"That I'm your black, fabulous bestie?"

"Yeah. Let's go with that."

Harper was glad to let P tell her about his night at the warehouse party. It distracted her briefly from the pain—and the idea that there was something wrong with the baby. The way the pain came, it felt how some women described labor. But babies didn't come *this* early, did they? She didn't know.

P pulled up to the entrance to the ER and raced around to get her door. "You can't park here!" she said.

"Shut up. I'm walking you in, then I'll go move it."

"P?" she asked, and stopped. "What if ... what if something's wrong with the baby?" Tears trembled in her eyes.

"Nothing's wrong with the baby."

"You don't know," she said, and the tears started to pour.

"Come on," he said and began to lead her into the hospital. It was only then that she noticed he wore nothing beneath his assless chaps.

"Can I ... help you?" the receptionist asked. Even through Harper's tears, she could tell the woman did a commendable job of not reacting to P's appearance.

"My friend is pregnant. It's her first trimester. She's in a lot of pain, in her stomach."

She was happy to let P take the lead as she tried to stuff the tears down her throat. The nurse on duty leaned forward and looked at her. "What's the pain on a scale of one to ten, ten being the worst pain you've ever known."

"I don't—Jesus," Harper said as a fresh wave came over her. She spun away from P and vomited into the small trash bin. It was mostly liquid, but as she opened her eyes she realized there was no liner in the trash and it was mesh.

"I'll take her from here," the nurse said. She gestured for two other nurses in scrubs, and was eased into a wheelchair.

"I'll be right here!" P called.

It was like her dream, with the fluorescent lights overhead. Only this time, she was in a wheelchair and not a gurney. "It's okay if I can't have anesthesia," she said. She was partially aware that she wasn't making sense.

"Let's have the doctor take a look at you before we talk about next steps," one of the nurses said gently.

She was wheeled into a beige, boring, but sterile room. Unlike the dream, there were no rusty hedge trimmers on the counter. Just boxes of gloves and glass jars with tongue depressors and cotton balls.

"Harper? I'm Dr. Fredette." The doctor looked too young to work in a hospital, and she'd appeared too quickly. *Where was the long wait?*

"What's wrong with me?" she asked. The room was too bright, too clean.

"That's what we're going to find out. Don't you worry, we're going to take good care of you. Are you dizzy? Can you stand?"

"Yeah, no, I'm not dizzy. I can stand."

"Can you put this gown on for me? Open in the back. I'll just step outside for a minute, okay?"

"Okay." When the doctor closed the door, Harper stood and stripped off the tank top and pajamas. It was cold in the exam room and the thin gown didn't provide any warmth. Goosebumps popped up on her flesh and the sound of the paper that crinkled beneath her as she sat on the exam table was too loud.

Harper dug through her purse for her phone. It was dead. *Fuck. I must have not plugged it in all the way.*

She tried not to cry as she waited for the doctor to return. *I should have told Sean,* she thought. *Now he'll wake up to that note, I'll be gone, and he won't have any idea what happened. I didn't even tell him which hospital.*

Finally, the knock came. "Alright, let's take a look and see what we can find out," the doctor said.

23

SEAN

Sean rolled over onto his back and pressed his palms into his eyes. The phone vibrated incessantly on his bedside table. It was still mostly dark outside. *It better be a goddamned emergency, whoever it is,* he thought to himself. As he reached for the phone, he sensed a vast openness next to him. *Where's Harper?* He was instantly awake.

He didn't recognize the number, but scrambled to answer it. "Hello?" he asked.

"Sean? It's P, Harper's friend."

"Are you with her?" he asked. "Where are you? What time is it?" Before P could answer, he lowered the phone to check the time. Four o'clock in the morning.

"*She's* okay," P said. "At least, the last I was told. "I took her to Cedars-Sinai."

"You took her? When? We were asleep—"

"She called me a couple of hours ago to come pick her up."

"What? Why did she call you? She was right here—"

"Look, I don't really know about that. I told her to wake you up, I told her to tell you, but you know how she can be. She told me she left you a note."

"A note? Why—what happened? What's wrong?" Sean bolted from bed and began to pull on a pair of jeans in the dark, the phone cradled precariously under his chin.

"I haven't been told much, and I won't be since I'm not family. But she's fine, and from what I understand the baby is fine. At least for now, but it's something to do with the pregnancy."

"You know about the baby?" Sean stopped his struggle with the balled-up jeans and stood still.

"I think I'm the only one she told besides you," P said gently. "I don't want to come down on you right now, and I know Harper's told me you've been doing a lot better with the whole normie thing of monogamy or whatever, but you need to figure your shit out."

"I'm trying," Sean said. He put down the phone briefly to pull on a t-shirt.

" ... how rare what you've got it? She shouldn't have to feel like she needs to call me in a crisis. You need to man up and be whatever she needs so she feels safe with you."

"I know, I know," Sean said. "I'm going to lose you in the stairwell. I'm coming now."

"Yeah, well," P said with a huff in his voice. "I'll be here."

Sean raced through the night. As he whipped into the parking lot, the morning sun had just started to struggle up the horizon. He saw P as soon as he walked in, draped in a black leather ensemble with his chest drenched in glitter. "Don't ask," P said, as he stood up to give Sean a brief hug and kiss on the cheek.

"Are ... one of you the father?" Sean turned around to see a doctor with dark circles under his eyes. His white coat was rumpled and he gripped a clipboard like it could save him.

P looked at Sean. "Oh. That's me, I am," he said. That would take some getting used to. *The father.*

"Harper's okay," the doctor said. "Though still a bit tired and confused from the pain medication."

"And the baby?"

"The fetus is viable," the doctor said as he glanced at his chart. "But Harper's had a placental abruption, which caused some internal bleeding. There was also some blood in her fluids."

Sean's breath was shaky. "Can I see her?"

"Of course. Just bear in mind that stress is the worst thing for her right now. Follow me."

P gave his forearm a squeeze as Sean started to trail after the doctor. "I'll be right here," he said. "Apparently I'm supposed to stay seated. My outfit seems to have offended some people."

The doctor held back a thin blue curtain for Sean like he was about to present him with a new car or an oversized check. Harper was tucked into the bed, her right arm and hand set up with IVs. She looked tiny, like a child.

"Harper?" he asked quietly, and her eyes fluttered open.

"Sean? I'm so sorry," she said. Her voice was hoarse and choked with tears.

He rushed to her side and did his best to carefully hug her. With his face buried into her neck, he felt the sting of tears threaten to fall. Seeing her like that was a blunt reminder of all he had to lose. "Don't be sorry," he whispered. "You have nothing to be sorry for. I'm sorry, I'm the one who should be sorry."

"No," she said, her voice tight. "I thought I could save the baby."

"You did," he said. "You did save the baby. The baby's fine."

"That's not what I meant," she said. "I thought it wasn't too late. That, you know, the rehab would work. I could fix myself—"

Sean leaned up and brushed a stray lock of fiery hair from her face. "I just talked to the doctor," he said. "He says the baby's hanging in there. You did good, you did the right thing."

"No," she said with a stubborn shake of her head. "I don't even know if you want the baby," she said. A fresh flood of tears started to trickle down her face. "And I don't blame you," she said. "It's not your fault. I go and bombard you with this news, you don't get a say in it. And it's not like we were *together* together or anything. I'm so fucking stupid—"

"Hey," he said as he tucked the hair behind her ear. "It's okay. Of course I want the baby. It's a piece of you, of course I want it." He kissed her softly and tasted the salt on her lips. "I'll take you in any form I can get."

Harper's body began to rock with the sobs, but this time she squeezed him back.

A nurse came in, plump with brown skin that looked soft as whipped butter. "You must be the father," she said with a warm smile. "Harper's a trooper. I just need to change up her pain meds, I won't be a minute," she said.

Harper let out a groan. "They make me too tired," she protested, though she knew it was useless.

"You need your sleep. That's what will make you stronger," the nurse said.

"It doesn't hurt," Harper said.

"It doesn't hurt because you're on pain meds," the nurse said with a small laugh. "In LA, let me tell you, this is a rarity. Someone comes into the ER in the middle of the night and doesn't want pain meds. That's what a lot of people come in here for."

Sean watched the nurse deftly swap out one of the bags. A fresh, strong fluid started to make its way into Harper's arm.

"It's going to make me fall asleep," Harper said apologetically to Sean.

"It's okay, you go ahead and sleep. I'll be right here when you wake up. P's here, too, but they're making him wait up front."

He thought Harper nodded, but she fell asleep so quickly he couldn't tell.

"Sorry," the nurse said. "She'll be much better when she wakes up after this dose, though."

"It's alright. Can I stay in here while she sleeps?"

"Sure, but it might be quite awhile," the nurse said. "Consider the chair yours."

He slumped into a hard, straight-backed chair and watched

Harper sleep. Sean matched her deep breaths with his. His head spun. *The father.* He'd never considered being a father before. But he had to admit, a little version of Harper could never be a bad thing. A little boy or girl with a head of fire and those deep eyes of hers that spilled over with curiosity.

Sean took in her sleeping form and reached out to touch her abdomen. It was still flat. He could tell even below the thin hospital blankets. It was their baby in there, strong as she was, whether he was ready for it or not.

He closed his eyes and let the darkness encircle him. The beeps from the monitors got louder and the scent that all hospitals had poured into him. *Please God, let her be okay. Let the baby be okay. Please, God.*

Sean couldn't remember the last time he'd prayed, unless he counted the prayers in his meetings with Joon-ki. But he was on autopilot with those, and had never really embraced the whole higher power aspect of Alcoholics Anonymous. Part of him felt like a fake for asking God, or whatever might be out there, for help now. *But if not now, when?*

Please, God, if you're out there ... I know I don't deserve this. I don't deserve Harper, or the baby, or anything else good. But she doesn't deserve this either. Please just let them be okay. Just let everything be okay.

Harper murmured in her sleep and his eyes opened. The brightness of the hospital room was nearly blinding. "It'll be okay," he told her quietly. "Don't worry about anything. You and the baby will be okay. We'll all be alright."

She made a sound that he thought was contentment and he closed his eyes again. *I know all the steps, all the stages. I know this is bargaining, and I know you get it all the time. But this is different, because this isn't about me. It's about Harper and the baby. Please, just let them be alright.*

Sean listened to the footsteps that passed down the hall, the squeak of rubber soles on the tile floor polished to a dull shine. He felt the buckle of his jeans press into his abdomen, and was glad for the physical reminder of being in the world. But mostly, he listened to the hum and clicks of Harper's monitors and willed them to remain steady.

24

HARPER

*H*arper blinked her eyes open, but squinted against the fluorescence that shone in from the hallway. She felt the stiff, starched sheet over her and let out a small groan. *The hospital. You're in the hospital*, she reminded herself. *Fuck, that's right. Sean would be pissed as hell, worried, or both by now and there was no way to get ahold of him.*

She could feel drugs as they coursed through her system and could tell the fatigue she felt was enforced. Still, as she struggled to sit up and felt the pinch of IVs in her skin, she let out a gasp as she looked down her body. The otherwise bright white sheets were stained with a pool of blood that looked almost fake.

A scream built up in her throat. It sounded like an animal, but she couldn't stop. A nurse in scrubs with a print of teddy bears burst into the room with a doctor on her heels. "Calm down," the nurse repeated. "Calm down, we need to get the ultrasound set up to see what's going on here."

"The baby," she screamed. "It's the baby."

The nurse prepped the machine that had been pushed into the corner of the room and pulled the soiled blanket and sheet off of Harper with a snap. Cold air rushed over her skin, and she realized her legs were covered in the congealed, sticky redness. When the nurse pushed up her gown and began to smear the jelly across her stomach, Harper was briefly embarrassed of the underwear she wore. The lace trim was worn out. "Always wear good, clean underwear in case you're hospitalized," her mother had always said.

The doctor took the little handheld element that looked like the scanners at department stores. He pressed firmly into her abdomen while he kept an eye on the screen. The same thing had happened when she was admitted, and Harper hadn't been able to see much on the grainy screen then either.

"Is the baby okay?" she asked.

"Please keep still," the nurse said. Her voice was kind but firm.

"Is the baby okay?" Harper asked again.

The doctor gave a slight shake of his head. "I can't seem to find the fetus …"

Harper let out a cry that sounded even to her like prey that had been shot in the dark. Sean walked through the door, two coffee cups in hand along with a heavy paper bag of muffins. "What's going on?" he asked. "Is everything okay?"

"No," Harper choked out. "The baby … they can't find the baby."

"I'm sorry," the doctor said. He looked briefly at Harper, then at Sean. "Sometimes these things happen." He looked at his pager. "It was the first trimester, and that time can be quite delicate—"

"It was me," Harper said. "I did it. Or didn't," she corrected. The tears had turned silent, a quiet faucet she couldn't turn off. "The baby couldn't stay because of me."

"I'll let Nurse Connie clean you up," the doctor said. "And I'll be back in a little while to discuss your options."

"Options?"

"It was the first trimester and you lost quite a bit of blood, but it wasn't a traditional miscarriage," he said. "Most of the time, I recommend a D and C to ensure all the waste is purged from the body."

Harper flinched at the word. Purged. She'd never be able to escape it. "No," she said vehemently as she started to shake her head. "I'm not doing that. I want a second opinion. The baby was just here—"

"I'm sorry," the nurse said as she squeezed Harper's hand. "It's gone." Sean started to move toward her, but the nurse stopped him with a single look. "You can sit in the chair," the nurse said, "out of the way."

"You don't know!" Harper screamed at the nurse, the doctor, Sean, all of them. "Try it again."

"Honey, I'm sorry," the nurse said. The doctor was silent, but made small scratches on the chart that hung from the foot of Harper's bed.

"You're sorry?" Harper asked. Hysteria mixed with a macabre laugh in her voice. "You're sorry? What are you sorry for? What did you do?"

"You're young," the nurse said. "You can try again."

"I wasn't fucking trying the first time!" Harper said. "I don't want another baby, I want *this* baby. You don't fucking get it, it was my only chance—"

"Up the sedation," the doctor said bluntly.

"What? No!" Harper said. "You can't just knock me out—"

But it was too late. Her own weakness surprised her. As Harper raised her hand to keep the nurse away from the IVs, the nurse easily pinned her arm down. She couldn't do anything but watch as the fluids flooded her body faster. The faux sense of calm and exhaustion moved through her body like an electric blanket.

"Harper, stop," she heard Sean say. *Stop what?* "It's okay, just rest."

Rest. She was tired of being told to rest, to calm down, that everything was okay. *Everything is clearly not fucking okay*, she tried to say, but the words just echoed in the empty chamber of her head.

She felt familiar arms around her shoulders and breathed Sean in. His body eclipsed the painful bright light above her. Harper tried to fight off the drugs, but they were too strong. She heard nurses murmuring and smelled fresh sheets. Someone, somehow, had already cleaned off her legs. She pressed her thighs together like she always did in bed, aware that the thigh gap had disappeared as the hard mattress pushed against her flesh.

I'm sorry. I fucked up. I fucked everything up. The words didn't come out, but she prayed that Sean could still hear them. Even as the blackness crept closer around her, she scanned her body and realized something was missing. There was an emptiness, a space, that was spooned out from her center. *How can you miss someone who'd only been a whisper inside you?*

She'd been wrong for all those days. Maybe there hadn't been any kicks or swells of the stomach, but the baby had been there. She'd known him, through and through. *Him*, she thought to herself. *I didn't realize that until now.*

Harper felt a bustling of busy nurses around her. They worked around Sean, too. The steadiness of his arms kept her from drifting away into the wild unknown. The smell of bleach filled the air, and she felt gentle sponges across her skin.

" … in time to make the softball game …" one of the nurses murmured. Harper would have laughed if she could at the idiocy of it all. Here they were, changing out her bloody sheets with bits of her baby on them as they talked about finishing a shift in time to go to a game.

Probably one of their kids' games, she thought and it hit her. Her child was gone. Her only child. No matter what any of them said, no matter what Sean would say when the drugs wore off, she wouldn't "try" again. The first had been the only, and he'd been a miracle. And she'd ruined it all, and for what? So she wouldn't get fat.

"There's a difference between fat and pregnant," P had said. *Obviously, right?* But she hadn't fully believed that. She'd watched friends expand into happy motherhood and had never understood how they could do that. Especially the models, the actresses, how they could just give up their whole body for a wiggling little pink thing. But now she knew. *Why do I always have to figure everything out so late?*

The walls were black velvet and closed in tighter. "I love you," Sean whispered into her ear. He just kept repeating it. She tried to open her mouth to tell him again how sorry she was, how she loved him, too. But no matter how much she tried, nothing came out.

She wanted to tell him that she understood now. *Just give me another chance, a do-over, and I'll get it right.* She would eat right, exercise in moderation, rest and do everything else she was supposed to. She'd no longer obsess over getting just the right supplements, but go with her gut and just start it already. Anything it took, she would do.

The doctor could be wrong, she tried to tell herself, but she knew that was a lie. She'd been asleep when the baby had slipped away, and she hadn't even noticed. Harper would never forget the shock of those red sheets. So bright and cheery, it had been so wrong. *Where had everyone been?* she thought. She remembered Sean with those white paper cups and the little brown paper bag that seeped out oil from the café.

The baby had known. He'd waited until it was just the two of them to make his escape. And Harper hadn't been able to stop him, to keep him. Even on her back, with her thighs spread thick, she hadn't been able to clamp her legs shut tight enough to keep him safe. The thigh gap had done what it was supposed to do. It was an alley, a highway, that let the greatest thing that had ever happened to her make a getaway into the night.

"Does she have any other family?" she heard a nurse ask.

"Not really," Sean said. He hesitated. *Don't call my mom. Don't you let them call my mom.*

"Parents?"

"Uh, not really," Sean said. She was aware of her phone, dead in her purse, but all it would take was a slight recharge for anyone to scroll through it to find her mother's number.

"Okay," the nurse said. "Just checking."

Harper sighed internally, slightly comforted, and let the dark take her.

25

SEAN

Sean's back ached, but he'd grown used to it. The little plastic chair he'd camped out in since Harper fell asleep pushed against his spine and refused to give. *You have to give it props for that,* he thought. The chair was nothing if not determined. And it reminded him of all the pangs and groans that went along with life.

Nurses came in after thirty minutes and went through a series of checks and tests that he knew nothing about. They always told him she was stable and that the rest was good. There were moments her eyelids fluttered wildly in REM. During those times he gripped her hand and spoke soothing words to her. Sean could only imagine the kind of demons that roamed her nightmares.

He went back and forth to the waiting room to check in with P, though he never had any news. Finally, Sean urged him, "Go home. I'll call you as soon as she wakes up."

P had looked around wearily and held the steady gazes of children who took in his outfit with curiosity. "Maybe you're right," P said. "This outfit doesn't exactly translate to daywear."

Sean thought about texting Joon-ki or even Connor, but what could he say? There was no way he could talk to anyone without spilling why Harper was in the hospital to begin with. It might be half his child, but it was her body—and up to her whether she ever told anyone else or not.

Instead, he asked the nurse for a few pieces of paper from the copy machine and a pen. He lost himself in his imagination and dreamed up cloudless landscapes, magical creatures and beautiful scenery on the white blank sheets. The least he could do was create a miniature of a perfect world, one suitable for Harper and the baby that had gone.

There was a shift in the hum of the machines that made Sean look up. He'd just finished a pastoral landscape drenched with flowers drawn in aching detail. He imagined it to be the kind of place they might retire one day. Maybe in the English midlands, or some vast openness in the middle of the country he only knew in dreams.

Harper let out a soft moan and flexed her fingers.

"Hey," he said as he stood up and leaned over the bed. "Welcome back."

"What time is it?" she asked, groggy.

He glanced at the clock. "Almost three."

"In the afternoon?"

"Yep. You slept most of the morning. Which is good."

She tried to push herself into a seated position but flinched.

"Don't strain yourself," he said and propped an extra pillow below her.

"I'm sorry." They were the first clear words she said.

"No more sorries."

"I can't help it," she said. "I feel like I, you know, I failed. At the first task of motherhood. Keep the baby alive, that was it. That was all I had to do."

"You make it sound like that's easy. Or that you even had much control over it. Do you remember what the doctor said? These kinds of things happen all the time."

"They happen a lot more when you're underweight. Malnourished," she said. "God. I'm so sorry. I mean, I knew I had vitamin deficiencies. Anemia, all that. I hoped the prenatal vitamins would boost me back up, but—"

"You have no idea whether that had anything to do with it or not. And we'll never know. So why worry about it?"

The nurse walked in as Harper started to protest more. "There's our sleeping beauty," she said. Her smile had the familiar slight tinge of coffee stains from daily habits, the same all the staff had. "Feeling better?"

"I wouldn't put it that way," Harper muttered. "Can you tell me more? What happened—I mean, I know what happened. But why?"

"Harper—" Sean started, but she quieted him with a look.

"I need to know," she said. "Was it me? Did I do something? Or ... not do something?"

The nurse went about her tasks as she checked Harper's vitals and the machines. "Miscarriages are a lot more common than most people think," she said. "They're most often caused by chromosomal abnormalities. Now, don't let that worry you," she said. "Even if that is the cause, which we can't know, that in no way means that you won't have a slew of babies in the future with no complications. It could also be a bunch of other reasons. If and when you're ready to try again, it's always best to work with an OBGYN before you even start trying. You can get tests to see what challenges you might face, and that can certainly give you peace of mind and help make future pregnancies easier."

"Yeah, I don't know if I'll 'try' ever again," Harper said. Sean squeezed her hand.

"You might and you might not," the nurse said with a shrug. "All I can tell you for certain is it's pretty pointless to think about such a big decision right here, right now."

"Thank you," Sean said. He meant it. The idea of actually planning a pregnancy seemed a world away. Still, there was a distinct sense of loss in the room. He hadn't realized how much he'd wanted that baby, even under the circumstances.

"Yeah," Harper whispered. "Thanks. When can I leave?"

"The doctor will come in to talk to you about that," the nurse said. "I don't expect you to stay overnight, but a little longer just for observation might be in order. Rest, relax. The café here is pretty good if you're hungry—at least, relatively speaking," she said with a wink.

They both listened to the nurse's footsteps as she retreated down the hall.

"You know," Sean said carefully, "don't take this the wrong way. I'm devastated about the loss. Really. More so than I thought I would be. But there's a part of me that's also ... relieved."

"Relieved? Really?" Harper asked. She looked up at him with her doe eyes, but all he saw when he searched them was interest. There was no judgment.

"Yeah, kind of," he admitted. "Just a little. I don't think either of us were ready for that kind of responsibility. Not yet."

"Maybe you're right," she said. "I'd be lying if I said I didn't agree. I mean, I was ready to make the best of it. But if it were totally up to me, up to us, to plan for something like this, it would definitely be down the road. And when I was, you know. Healthier."

"Well, now it is completely up to us," he said.

"I guess so," Harper said. A slight smile played at her lips.

Sean sighed and pulled the chair beside her bed. "You know, I'm still counting the days since my relapse," he said. "I try not to talk about it much, and think about it even less. But the day will come when you just stop counting and can't remember off the top of your head how many days you've been sober. That's kind of a small sign for me. But that day is still a ways out."

"I'm sorry," she said. "I can't fathom what that's like."

"Sure you can," he said. "You're still in rehab. It might be for something totally different, but there are similarities. Alcohol's one kind of addiction, eating, or lack thereof, is kind of another."

"Yeah, I can see that," she said.

"With alcohol, the goal is to avoid it," he said. "In some ways, that's a little easier. But with you, with the eating disorder, it's about tackling it head-on every single day. You're so much stronger than I could be."

"Don't say that," she said. Harper squeezed his arm. "They're just different, but both monsters." She began to cry, slow and steady.

"Hey," he said softly. "What is it?"

She shook her head. "I know you're right," she said. "About everything, about the timing. About being relieved. But it still hurts. You know?"

"I know," he said. "Trust me, I know. And when we're ready, really ready, we'll try again. Okay? We can have ten kids if that's what you want."

"You mean it?" she asked.

"Here," he said and stretched out his hand. "Pinky swear."

"I'm not pinky swearing on ten kids. You're going to have to give my vagina some kind of break."

"Okay," he said. "We'll just swear on trying. And waiting until we're ready."

"Deal," she said and wound her finger around his.

"Are you hungry?" he asked. "You want me to go check out the café? I saw some of the food delivered to the room and it's not very impressive."

"Can we just sit here for a moment? Just, you know … observe the loss? I think, after that, I can start to put this behind us."

"Of course," he said. "Anything you want."

Sean eased back into the seat, and it finally gave. He'd

conformed to it, or maybe it was the other way around. But he felt cradled, and Harper's hand in his anchored him. He closed his eyes and listened to her breathe. Sean thought about how close they'd come to diving right into the deep end. It would have been scary, was scary, but also exhilarating.

You'll have another chance, a voice inside him whispered. Maybe it was his, maybe it wasn't. It was too quiet to tell.

When Harper squeezed his hand, he opened his eyes and looked at her. An open smile stretched across her face.

Sean stood up, leaned down and kissed her.

Harper wiped the last of the tears from her cheeks and nodded at him.

They didn't need words or any more explanations. He knew intuitively what that meant. They were ready, bound together by all they'd had and all they'd lost. Now, without reservations, they could move on—together—into the luminous.

26

HARPER

"Are you sure you're ready for this?" Sean asked. "You don't have to go in today if you don't want to."

She smiled over at him as the engine idled and purred below. She'd only been home a few days, but the cabin fever had enveloped her fast. Harper had been surprised when the first place she wanted to go was rehab, but it kind of did make sense. What she needed now was healthy support more than anything else. "I'm sure," she said.

"Okay," Sean said. "But if you want to leave early today, just give me a call. This is a lot, a full day after what you just went through."

"It'll be good for me," she said. "Promise."

He leaned over and pressed his lips against hers. Harper's mouth opened, receptive. There were no hesitations, which she'd worried about in the hospital. Instead, since the day he'd brought her home, it was as if they were closer than ever.

"Good luck, sweetheart," Sean called after her. She gave him an exaggerated eye roll over her shoulder and blew back a kiss.

"Harper!" the receptionist said. "So good to see you! We weren't sure you'd make it back in this week."

"Hi," Harper said. "I did. I'm here. It feels good to be back."

"It's good to have you back. The group's just settling in," she said.

As Harper made her way down the hall, one of her favorite doctors—a resident psychologist—turned the corner. "Harper, you're here," she said warmly. The young doctor always looked like she was playing dress-up in her lab coat. She had the smooth-skinned young face of a high schooler who had somehow escaped the curse of acne. "How are you feeling today?"

"Surprisingly good," Harper said.

"The staff has been updated on the past week's occurrences. I'm so sorry for your loss."

"Thank you." This was one of the things Harper had been afraid of. How would she react to sympathies and condolences? She didn't know if she'd be able to handle it, but hearing someone offer their wishes in earnest made the baby feel more like he'd been part of this world.

Harper ducked into the group room as the doctor gave her a gentle squeeze on the shoulder. "—go over the foundational —Harper! You made it to group, that's fantastic."

She blushed slightly as she made her way into the circle. Billy reached behind him, his willowy figure bending at fantastic angles, and pulled up a chair beside him. He patted it as the rest of the group members smiled at her. "Sit here," he said.

As she looked around the room, she realized nobody but the medical staff knew why she'd been gone. It wasn't odd to have someone disappear for a few days, or even for good. There was no telling what might happen. Harper had heard stories of some people leaving forever, only for an obituary to be stumbled across the following week. It was usually a sudden heart attack or a hip fracture. Starvation usually made your body consume its heart first after all the fat had been gobbled up. The bones were nearly hollow as a bird's and delicate as a soufflé.

Only the group leader offered Harper a smile of camaraderie that let her know she knew about the baby. "Harper, since it's your first day back, you get the choice of when you'd like to share today. If at all, of course."

Harper looked around the room at the motley crew of misfits. She drew in her breath. "I'm ... okay, I guess. Not great, not terrible."

"Why were you gone?" Billy asked. He leaned toward her, his eyes hungry for drama.

"Billy, you know we don't ask that," the group leader said.

"Too late," he said with an unapologetic shrug.

Harper laughed. His countenance reminded her of P. "It's okay," she said. "If I'm not going to share here, then where? I was in the hospital," she said.

Everyone nodded. They'd assumed that.

"I ... I miscarried. Everyone there said it's really common for women with eating disorders. Well, I mean, we all know that."

"I've had four," one of the girls said. Her oily hair hung in tired strands down her face.

"No competition," the group leader said. "This is about Harper right now."

"It was my first," Harper said. "The good thing, I think, is that the doctors and nurses weren't really adamant that it was because of my weight. They basically said it could happen for a million reasons."

"And how do you feel about the pregnancy ending?" the group leader asked.

"Sad," Harper said simply. She gave a short laugh. "That sounds juvenile, I know, but it's true. I … I really love the man who was the father. But, we talked about it. He's in recovery, too." The group leader raised her brow. "Alcohol, not an eating disorder. We both know it wasn't the right time or circumstances for a baby, so in a way I'm kind of glad I don't have to be pushed into being a mom right now. I know that sounds terrible. And selfish."

"There's nothing wrong with being selfish sometimes," the group leader said. "Our society reveres self-deprecation, false modesty, sarcasm—but there's nothing good in them most of the time. For a lot of us, that rewires our inner voice, or self-talk. We face enough negativity in the world. If our inner voice doesn't talk kindly to us, we start to believe it."

"Yeah," Harper said. "I know. But doesn't that make me a bad person? For being partly grateful to not have a baby right now? Even though it's a small part?"

"Nothing's black and white," Billy said.

"That's right," the group leader said. "Or at least, very few things are."

"I don't know," Harper said. She began to tear up. "I read some things? About the importance of thought and will during a pregnancy? What if ... what if the baby somehow knew he wasn't totally wanted?"

"Harper, I can promise you that a lot of women aren't one hundred percent sure about being a mother. Even the people who plan, who get IVF, who spent years and life savings on getting pregnant will have their doubts. If having doubts caused miscarriages, our species would be in serious trouble."

She wiped the tears from her cheeks. "I guess you're right. I—this sounds stupid, I know—but I know Sean and I are meant to be together. And to have a family ..."

"That doesn't sound stupid," the session leader said. "It sounds brave. And like you're looking toward a happy, healthier future."

"But it seems selfish, you know? To be so certain of him and our future together, but at the same time feel like it's not time to start a family. Let's be honest, we're both kind of a hot mess right now."

"You've talked about Sean before. You've known him, what, a couple of months?" the group leader asked.

"Yeah," she said softly. She knew how unbelievable it sounded, to be so sure of a soulmate you'd barely known for a few weeks.

"You've certainly gone through a lot in a short amount of time. That can either drive a new couple apart or bond them closer together. It sounds like you're heading down the latter path."

Harper gave her an appreciative smile. "How did Sean take it?" Billy asked.

"Perfectly," she said. "I was kind of out of it, with the drugs at the hospital and all. I mean, he was sad, too, but also relieved."

"My last miscarriage was just last year," the mousy girl said. "I know! I know, it's not about me," she said before the group leader could reel her in. "I just wanted to tell you, if you ever want to talk? Like, one-on-one? I'm here. Sorry if I sounded like I was trying to lessen what you went through."

"Thanks," Harper said. "I might take you up on that sometime."

"Well, Harper, it's great to have you back," the group leader said. "Why don't we take a short break from sharing and let's open our food journals."

Harper watched everyone else as they dug out their tattered Moleskines and composition books. Some of them had decorated their journals with sketches and stickers from favorite coffee shops, or outlines of their home state. Others had chosen nondescript journals that wouldn't encourage anyone to pry.

"Sorry," she said. "I didn't really keep a journal in the hospital. But I can guarantee you that I ate all my jello."

"Ugh," Billy said. "If there's anything that's going to inspire a relapse into anorexia, it's hospital food. They should market that as the ultimate diet."

As she surveyed the room with everyone busily bookmarking pages and comparing cheat meals, a warmth settled inside her. This room, these people, it felt good. Everyone was right—therapy wasn't easy. It was hard, sometimes almost impossible. Relearning how to think about her body, herself, and food was going to take a lifetime of management. But so far, it was worth it.

"How many calories do you think is in a fried egg made with just, like, a tiny bit of Pam spray?" somebody asked. "Like, the calories on the Pam can say zero, but it's for a tiny amount. How can it be olive oil *and* no calories? And how can an egg gain calories just by being cooked? That's so weird, and totally not fair. Raw eggs are gross. I never got that—"

"You know food journal shares aren't for talking about calories or assigning a number to the food," the group leader said. "We need to learn to look at, talk about, and think about food differently."

"I know that," the girl said huffily. "I was just wondering. It's, like, a science question."

"Honey, do we look like scientists?" Billy asked.

27

SEAN

Sean stared at his phone. His thumb had hovered over Ashton's name for the past twenty minutes. *He probably won't even answer*, he thought. It was the first day Harper had driven herself to therapy since the hospital. She'd be gone the entire day. He'd tried to hype himself up for the call, but every time he went to press the green call button something inside him froze.

Don't be such a pussy, he told himself. *It'll just go to voicemail anyway.*

Finally, Sean pressed the call button. His heart began to race as he listened to the rings.

"What do you want?" Ashton asked coldly. "You know it's dangerous—for you—to talk to me rather than have your attorney call mine."

"Can we talk?" Sean asked. He forced out the question before he could second-guess himself.

"I believe that's what we're doing."

"I mean in person. Can we meet up?"

Ashton gave a short, mean laugh. "What for?"

"Look, I just really think we need to talk. If you're still mad at me afterward, you can kick my ass."

"I don't need your permission for that," Ashton said.

"Maybe not, but can we at least be civil beforehand?"

Ashton sighed. "You're lucky you caught me after my PT. I'm in a generous mood. Okay, I'll give you twenty minutes."

"Great, thanks," Sean said. He hated himself for thanking Ashton, but it had been such a surprising win that he couldn't find his right bearings. "How about Blackwood?"

"Blackwood?" He thought he heard Ashton take a long draw on a cigarette. "Didn't know you were some basic bitch now. But alright. I can be there in an hour."

Sean faced the windows of the coffee shop. He couldn't stop his right leg from shaking violently under the table, a nervous habit from his childhood he'd never been able to get rid of. Finally, he saw Ashton make his way across the street. He had a bad limp, but that was to be expected. What he didn't expect was just how fucked up Ashton looked in the middle of the day.

Ashton barreled into the coffee shop. The dark vintage Ray-Bans couldn't hide the manic high he was on. The temperature hovered near seventy-five, but Ashton was sweating like it was a sauna. His skin looked pale and pocked, and as Sean stood up to greet him he caught a strong whiff of bourbon. "Hey," Sean said. "Thank you for meeting me."

Sean reached his hand out to Ashton, and when his old friend took it out of habit, he noticed fresh track marks on his arm. The cuticles had been chewed until they'd bled. Rusty, dried red streaks nestled into the fingernails. "Well?" Ashton said. His voice sounded strange, high and frantic. "Gimme your speech. I know you have one prepared."

"I'm sorry," Sean said. "That's not much of a speech, I know, but it's honest and it's all I've got. I'm sorry for it all. For that night, for—"

"Sorry for fucking around with my girl? What about that, huh?" Ashton's voice was tinged with anger, but his gaze flew around the shop like a madman.

"What?"

"She fucking left me, man. She—"

"Wait, are you still hung up on her?" Sean hadn't expected that. The so-called girlfriend had been a booty call for Ashton at best, and one of many. She'd been Sean's girlfriend first, though he'd been more than happy to pass her along to Ashton. He shook his head at the memories. *To think that's what you used to think a relationship was.*

"Of course I am! Fuck, man, what did you think?"

"Have you ... have you seen her? Since, you know ..."

"No. She doesn't want anything to do with me. Not that you'd give a damn. Does that make you happy? Hold up, are *you* with her? Is that what this is all about?" Ashton slammed his palms down on the table and leaned toward Sean.

"What? No. I'm with—well, never mind. Why won't she talk to you?"

"Because she's fucking sober," Ashton said. "Okay? Is that what you want to hear?"

"Getting sober is hard work. A lot of people will tell you not to get into any kind of romantic relationship when you're—"

"I offered to get sober, too. For her," Ashton said.

"Really?" Sean wished he could take back the surprise in his voice. He didn't know how serious Ashton was about that, but simply saying it seemed like a big step. Of course, it was never a good idea to try and get sober for somebody else, but it was a common first step a lot of addicts in recovery took.

"You think I'm making this bullshit up?"

"Why don't you sit down, Ashton?" Sean asked gently.

"I don't want to fucking sit down! She said—she said even if I was sober, she didn't want me back. Because she, you know, her and I got together while she was with someone else. Said it didn't comment well on my character, or some shit."

"Okay," Sean said. "It doesn't really reflect well on her, either. But ... what if I call her? Put in a good word for you? I mean, you'd have to get clean—"

"You wouldn't do that for me," Ashton said.

"I would, if it meant that you were really going to call off this whole lawsuit." *Is that really what this whole thing has been about?* Some girl, one that Sean could hardly remember? And if he could hardly remember her, and he'd been her alleged boyfriend, how much stock could Ashton really have in her? He'd always been more fucked up than Sean was.

But Ashton sat down and slowly took off the sunglasses. Sean willed himself not to wince at the sight. Ashton's eyes were bloodshot and the dark circles under his eyes looked like they'd been dug by a gravedigger. "I look like hell, I know," Ashton said. There was a hint of his old friend in the haggard voice. "Fuck, I don't know," he said. "I don't know!"

Sean wanted to say more. He'd beg, he'd do nearly anything to get all of this over with. He knew Ashton, though, and he didn't do well with being pushed.

"Okay," Ashton said finally. He said it with his head hung low, but he said it. "Okay."

"I can't … look, Ashton, I can't promise anything," Sean said. "But I'll try. I'll call her, and I'll do my best. But I'm serious, you have to get clean, too. If she's sober, then there's no way she'll take you back if you're not on the wagon, too."

"Yeah, yeah," Ashton said. "I know."

"And here's the other part of the deal," Sean said. It was a risk, to push this hard, but he had to do it. "If you drop the charges, I'll talk to her but you have to come to a meeting, too."

"A meeting?" Ashton raised his brow at Sean. "Like some of that 'my name is Dickhead and I'm an alcoholic' type of bullshit?"

"Yeah, that kind of bullshit," Sean said. "But, you know, if you take it seriously? It helps. I know it sounds really LA enlightening and all, but it works. The meeting I go to, it has a good mix of people. Not what you'd expect."

"Huh," Ashton said. Sean didn't know what that meant, but Ashton pulled out his phone. "I can call my lawyer right now," Ashton said. "If you call her."

Sean blew out his breath but began to scroll through his own phone. He knew there was a reason he hadn't yet bothered to delete all the numbers from his past life. He'd been worried that Harper might one day see his phone and wonder at all the names, but know he knew it was Ashton he'd held out for. Not anybody else.

"You first," Ashton said. "Put it on speakerphone."

"Speaker—are you serious?" Sean asked. "Here?"

"I won't say anything."

Sean knew he couldn't trust an addict, but it was the only shot he had. As the rings began, he put it on speakerphone and placed his phone on the table between them.

"Hello?" she sounded wary, as she should. He didn't know if she'd looked him up at all since the accident. For all she knew, he could be drugged out and sleeping on the street.

"Hey, hi," he said. "How's ... how's it going?"

"Sean? Uh, fine. Why are you calling me?"

"Honestly? It's about Ashton."

She gave a deep sigh. "What did he do now? You know I have zero contact with him, I don't know why you're calling me."

She was angry, and maybe rightfully so. "Look, I'll just lay this out straight for you. I ... I know he wants you back. And I heard you're sober now, which is great. I'm in AA, too—I mean, I don't know if that's part of your recovery. So I know it's discouraged to date someone who's an alcoholic, but ... I just wanted to tell you he's cleaning himself up. He really loves you. And, well, I just wanted to say you should think about giving him a second chance."

"Did he put you up to this?"

Ashton gave him a look. "No. I mean, he's talked to me about you, yeah. But I'm being real. He's a good guy, deep down. And he cares about you."

"Ugh, Sean, I don't know. This is weird! You and I used to be together. Kind of, you know. And he's really fucked up. Like, really, really fucked up. More than you and I ever were. With the drugs and all, you know, that's a whole other element."

"I know, I understand," he said. "But can I be honest with you? I'm with someone now. She's not an alcoholic or a drug addict, but she has her own issues, too. We all do. But when you find someone who really gets you, that you connect with? That's hard to find. I just, you know, I wish you'd give Ashton another chance."

"You really think he's a good guy?" she asked. "For real."

"I do," he said. And realized he meant it.

"Okay," she said.

"Really?"

"Yeah. I mean, if he gets clean and stays that way, who knows? If I'm being honest, I've never stopped caring about him."

"Well, that's great. Thanks. Take care of yourself, okay?"

"I'm trying." She hung up without saying goodbye.

"Thanks," Ashton said. Sean thought he heard a tightness in his voice. "I, uh, I'm going to call my lawyer, then."

"Thank you," Sean said. "So … I guess if that's that, I'll get going. I have a girlfriend waiting at home."

"Lucky you," Ashton said. "Hey, Sean?"

Sean turned around with his hand on the door. "Yeah?"

"I wish you luck in the future. I really do."

Sean smiled. "I don't need luck. I've got my girl, got a job. That's all I need. But thank you, anyway."

As he walked toward his car, there was a lightness in him he hadn't felt in years.

28

HARPER

"You look great," Sean said. He came up from behind her and wrapped his arms around her waist. "Like a serious girlboss."

"Hah," Harper said. "I'll be thrilled at assistant, gofer, coffee-getter or any other menial title Sophia might feel inclined to throw my way."

"She'd be insane not to hire you," he said. "Especially in this outfit, goddamn."

"Stop it!" she said with a giggle. "This is couture."

"Whatever it is, it's working," he said.

Harper pulled delicately at the hem of the fitted dress. It had been a gift from a designer after she'd headlined his spring runway show. At the time, she'd been excited to get it, but had also considered it just another perk of the business. *If I'd only known this would be the last couture I'd walk in.*

"You want me to drive you?" he asked.

"No, I'm okay. No offense, but I don't want her to see me being dropped off like it's my first day of school."

"None taken. But I think the dress is missing something."

"What?" She scanned herself in the mirror, but didn't see anything missing.

"Maybe a little accessorizing?" he asked. Sean held up the rose gold collar he'd gifted her what seemed like a lifetime ago.

"Sean," she said with a blush. "How'd you find that?"

"You didn't exactly hide it," he said. She lifted up her hair to let him attach the thin clasps together.

"It's perfect," she said. Harper ran her hand across the wisp of a collar. Anyone else would think it was a feminine choker. She liked this, a secret in plain sight.

Sean kissed her neck and caught her gaze in the mirror. "Go get 'em," he said.

Harper's heart fluttered as she entered the hotel bar drenched in natural light. She scanned the room in search of the face she'd memorized from Sophia's professional headshot. However, she would have picked her out from a crowd even without the photo. There was no way to overlook a former model. The older woman screamed sophistication as she smiled up at the waiter who brought her a club soda.

"Harper," Sophia said as Harper approached the table. "You look even lovelier in person."

"Thank you for meeting me, Mrs.—"

"Please, call me Sophia," she said. "Sit. I was thinking a white wine, but I wanted to wait and see if you'd like to join me."

"Uh, sure," Harper said.

"Two glasses of your driest white, and the olives," Sophia said. "So," she said as she leaned toward Harper. "I know this isn't the West Coast way of doing things, but I'm a New York girl. Thus the black suit. Tell me about yourself."

"Well, I started with a jeans campaign when I was—"

"No. Tell me about yourself," Sophia said again. The waiter presented two chilled glasses of wine and swiftly moved away.

"I've been in outpatient recovery for about a month now," Harper said. "Anorexia and bulimia. There were a few days I missed because ... well, because I had a miscarriage and was hospitalized."

"I'm sorry to hear that," Sophia said.

You're so stupid. Way to let a potential boss know you're totally unstable. "Thank you," she said. "I hope this doesn't come off as crass but, given the circumstances, my partner and I have decided it's a bit of a blessing in disguise. We're young, there's a big future ahead of us."

"And how is the therapy going? For the eating disorder?" Sophia sipped her wine but didn't break her gaze with Harper.

"It's going," Harper said. "Like many in the ED community, I consider it possible to manage an eating disorder for life, but not necessarily recover. A bit like alcoholism, I suppose. Of course, ED is a mental disorder, not necessarily an addiction unless you're talking about some cases of binge eating disorder or night eating syndrome. Still, there are definitely elements of similarity."

"You talk like a professional," Sophia said. "About your eating disorder, I mean."

Harper blushed slightly. "I'd hardly consider myself a professional," she said. "But it seems once a person is solidly on a path to management, they really immerse themselves in the research and best practices." She shrugged. "It's just a byproduct of incredible self-retrospection, I suppose."

Sophia nodded. "I agree. And I'm glad you're getting help."

But, Harper thought. *Here comes the big, fat but. Why'd I have to go into all of this? I totally blew it.*

"In fact," Sophia said, "I want you to *be* the help. For young models who need it most. I know we talked previously a little about potential job opportunities for you within my company, but I have something else in mind."

"Something else?"

"What do you think about being an eating disorder educator for young models? It's a new idea I've been thinking about for awhile, and I believe you're perfect for it. For now, it would be part-time, though I can certainly see the potential for it growing into a full-time position. You'd be able to work in just about any city, so long as you don't mind traveling some. It's especially great that you're in Los Angeles, one of the biggest modeling hubs in the world. I envision you outreaching to up-and-coming models, particularly young women and girls who are thrust into this often vicious industry without any kind of support or foundation."

"I ... I'm flattered," she said. "But, you know, I don't have any formal training in eating disorders. I'm far from a psychologist or any kind of specialist."

"But you have something even better," Sophia said. "Personal experience. And young girls, they don't want some dried-up, boring psychologist telling them what they should be thinking and feeling about themselves. They need someone they can relate to, and someone who's been in their shoes. Empathy is one of the most challenging skills to learn, but you've already got it in spades. I can see that."

"I wasn't expecting this," Harper said. The cold wine shot straight from her tongue to her belly. It infused her with just the right amount of liquid courage she needed. "I'd love to do it," she said. "In a few months."

"A few months?" Sophia cocked her head.

"Yes, if that's at all possible. Perhaps October? I just … I think I need to explore my own path to management a little more first. And, you know, as long as my boyfriend thinks it's a good idea. He's been a key part of my getting better."

"I see," Sophia said. "Harper, I have to tell you, that was either a really stupid move or a gutsy one. Few people in your position would try to leverage for a later start date. But I like you. I know we just met, but I have a good feeling about you. You practice self-care, and that's exactly what these girls you'd be mentoring need to learn. I can give you until October, but I'd need you to do some prep work before then. Developing strategies, helping to create your team, those sorts of tasks. Are you up for it?"

"Yes," Harper said. "I believe I am. But can I give you a firm answer on Friday? I need to think it over a bit more."

"You drive a hard bargain," Sophia said with a smile. "I like that."

Harper drove home full of excited energy.

"Hey!" Sean said. "How'd it go? Did your collar bring you luck?"

"It did," she purred as she nuzzled up to him. "Sophia wants me to be an ED educator for young models. Totally different than what she'd originally planned, but I'm excited for it. You know? I can maybe, this is clichéd, but make a difference. Keep at least one girl from going down the path I did."

"That's awesome, sweetheart," he said as he pulled her against his chest. "Congratulations."

"So you think it's a good idea?"

"Of course I do! And, hey, I'm not trying to upstage your good news, but I have some of my own."

"What's that?"

"I officially accepted Connor's job offer."

"Seriously?"

"Seriously. Although, I'm going to keep working a few days a month at a tattoo shop, too."

"You're going back to Mission Hells?"

"Not exactly," he said. "Joon-ki told me about this shop that caters exclusively to sober people. They offer pro bono work to cover up tattoos with drug- or alcohol-related ink and gang tattoos, too. I figured that could be my creative outlet, and maybe snap up some good karma points, too."

"That's amazing," she said. "I'm so proud of you. Hey, do you think I could draw a tattoo?"

"On me?"

"No! I mean, in general," she said.

"Sure. Anyone could," he said.

"So … I've been kind of doodling? You know, in group sessions—"

"Show me," he said.

"Don't laugh!" Harper dug the notebook out of her bag and handed it to him.

"A heart?" he asked.

"Kind of. It's the official symbol of supporting eating disorder management. The fluid lines, they're part heart and part a healthy body image."

"I love it," he said. "Do you want me to help refine it a little bit?"

"I think it needs all the help it can get."

"Not really," he said as he leaned down to kiss her. "It just needs a little help. How about we give it some more depth? Maybe add some color?"

She rested her head on his shoulder as he brought her little heart to life.

29

SEAN

"And over here, we have the atrium." Sean followed the broker to a glassed-in area in the middle of the space. Sunlight poured through the ceiling. The broker flicked her fingers across a control panel and a sheath of tinted curtain started to slide across the skylights. "You can control all the skylights and windows in the space with an app, too, of course," she said. "The one previous client used the atrium for corporate yoga classes every morning."

"What do you think?" Sean asked. He looked over at Harper.

She scanned the sleek, midcentury modern office space. "I think it's perfect," she said. "The furniture, too."

"I helped the previous client secure the furniture," the broker said. "And I can promise you the furnished rate is an absolute steal. Almost all of the furniture is from local carpenters and designers. It's the highest quality and, given the style, has incredible evergreen potential."

Sean wrapped his arm around Harper. "Is it alright if we just hang out here for awhile?" he asked the broker.

"Of course! I'll text you the code to lock up when you're finished. But I should tell you, and this isn't a sales tactic, if you want it I highly recommend you sign today. You're the last person viewing it until tomorrow, but I don't see it lasting on the market for long."

"Thanks," Sean said. "I'll let you know either way this afternoon."

He waited until they heard the click of the broker's heels fade into quiet before he squeezed Harper and pulled her against his chest. "Tell me what you really think," he whispered.

"What I really think? I think … I can see us both working here."

"Did Connor offer you a job I don't know about?"

"No," she said. Harper nudged his chest with her chin. "I mean, Sophia said I can work from anywhere, and an office space would be a tax write-off anyway. So I was thinking … maybe I could lease one of the offices here."

"You wouldn't get sick of me?" he asked. "Seeing me every day at home and work both?"

Harper laughed. "I think if I was going to get sick of you, it would have happened when you were sporting that hot ankle bracelet and we were basically housebound together."

"You might be right about that," he said. "But don't think I didn't know when you made up excuses to stay out of the house more than was necessary."

"You caught me," she said. "But then again, the circumstances were a little bit different back then."

"Not completely. One thing about our relationship has always been the same."

"What's that?" she asked as she looked up at him.

"No matter what was going on between us, or if I had an ankle bracelet or not, the sex was always fucking incredible."

Harper blushed slightly. "What can I say? Ankle bracelets do it for me."

"So, you're absolutely sure about this place? Buying commercial space is a much bigger deal than leasing it."

"I'm sure," she said.

"Okay, that's all I needed to hear. We'll put in an offer now. But don't be talking about leasing a space from me. You know it's yours. Ours. Everything is, from this point on."

They walked side by side through the atrium and into the sprawling open reception space. The marble tiled floors featured just the slightest of gray veins. Harper ran her hand across the long welcome desk with the thick living edge wooden top. "Aren't we supposed to shake hands or something?" she asked. She looked up at him coyly.

"That seems a bit formal," he said. "How about this instead?" Sean leaned down to meet her lips. Harper parted her mouth and eagerly welcomed his tongue. Before he closed his eyes, he saw the view of Los Angeles roll out before them. From the top floor, ten stories up, the magic of the city seemed anew. Palm trees swayed gently in the wind and the Hollywood sign peeked out of the green.

Harper let out a moan into his mouth as his hands slid down to her ass and squeezed firmly. As the tip of her tongue met his, he lifted her onto the reception desk. She struggled to open her legs, to pull him close, but the close cut of the skirt left her trapped. Sean gripped the hem of her skirt and tested the material.

She responded to his kisses, starved for more. "Please fuck me," she whispered.

"Are you sure?" he asked. This kind of heat hadn't boiled between them since before the hospital.

"Fuck me right now," she demanded.

Sean easily ripped the material and created a slit in the skirt from her knee to her hip. As soon as she could part her legs, Harper dug her nails into his back and pressed him against her. Sean reached between her legs and was met with the heat of her folds, already slick with her wetness.

"No panties," she said and smiled into his mouth.

"You're full of surprises." He hooked a finger around the rose gold collar and brought her mouth closer to his. With his other hand, he circled her opening until she wiggled in frustration. "Stop," he said hoarsely. "I think you're forgetting who's in charge here." He pulled firmly on her collar and her eyes opened.

"Yes, sir," she said.

"Lie back," he said. He released her and unbuckled his jeans while she moved back on the table. "Spread your legs, hold them open," he said.

Harper glanced briefly out the glass windows. Neighbors in nearby buildings could be seen as they bustled about in suits and dresses.

"Are you going to obey?" he asked, the belt buckle in hand.

Harper looked down at the metal in his fist, at the thick leather band, and held her thighs wide. Spread-eagle on the desk, she propped herself up on her elbows and watched him release his cock. Without thought, she bit her lower lip in desire.

"Now," he said, as he bent forward and easily tore the white silk blouse out of the waistband of her white skirt, "you're going to do as I say." He tore open the flimsy material and hardened more at the display of her bare breasts. "You have been naughty today," he said. "No bra either. Were you planning this?"

Harper's eyes widened. "Not really ... I mean—"

"Quiet," he said. Sean slid his hand beneath the tightness of her collar and engulfed her porcelain neck in his hand. "You might not be able to speak much to use your safe words," he said. "Tap my elbow if you want me to stop. Understand?"

"Yes, sir," she said.

He increased the pressure slightly on her neck as he entered her. Sean could feel the moan in her throat. It vibrated into his hand. She was wetter than he'd ever seen her as he controlled her breath. When he looked down to watch his length slide into her pink center, he almost gasped at the rivers of wetness that rushed down her thighs and onto the rich warmth of the desk.

Harper kept her hands on her thighs to force them as open to his thrusts as possible. Sean sensed when she was close and pressed his thumb into her swollen clit. "Come for me," he told her. She obeyed immediately. Halfway through her orgasm, he released her neck and she let out a low, animal keen. The sound was so wild, so naturally a part of her, that it forced him to come inside her. She clutched at his hips when she felt the release and pulled him deeper inside her.

"I think I ruined your table," she said with a small laugh as he pulled out of her. Sean watched his come begin to spill out of her and onto the wood.

"I guess I really do have to buy it now, sweetheart," he said. Sean leaned down to kiss her. "It's a good thing I love you."

"I love you, too," she said. He pulled her up and she guiltily looked out the window to check for an audience. If anyone had seen, they pretended otherwise. She laughed. "Did you ever think we'd be here?"

He brushed some loose strands from her face. "I didn't expect any of this," he said. "But I have to say, even with all our hardships, I couldn't have hoped or dreamed of anything better."

Harper wrapped her arms around him, pulled him close, and rested her head on his chest.

From his darkest depths, his most secret of places, Sean's heart swelled in a way he'd never known.

30

HARPER

TWO WEEKS LATER

"I don't know why you're doing this!" Harper said with a laugh. "It's just one month."

"One month of continuous rehabilitation is a big deal, it's worth celebrating," Sean said. "And it would have been longer if it wasn't for—well, you know."

"Yeah, I know," Harper said. "But everything worked out as it should."

"Is it going to feel strange? Not going there almost every day?" he asked.

Harper toyed with the diploma her doctor had presented to her. One month of more than full-time outpatient rehabilitation meant she'd continue with weekly or biweekly check-ins for several months. However, for the most part she was on her own, equipped with the tools and skills she'd need to guide her own lifetime of management. "Kind of," she admitted. "It'll be hard to lose that kind of nonstop support. But good that I'm getting weaned before I become dependent on it."

Sean finished taping the last streamer to the exposed pipe of the ceiling. As he climbed down the small ladder, she watched his muscles work below his thin t-shirt. Harper clutched the diploma tighter. That little piece of paper and what it represented had saved so much. She'd never have this, never have him, if it weren't for it. "Well, that's it," he said. "Last chance. Are you sure you don't want to have the entire party here?"

Harper bit her lip and shook her head. "I've been craving sushi for two months," she said. "I mean, basically since I couldn't have it."

"I can't believe we managed a table at Sushi of Gari," Sean said. "It was meant to be. Someone out there really thinks you deserve it." He leaned over and kissed her head as he passed the couch. "And I agree. Ready in fifteen?"

Harper touched up the loose waves that hung down to her stomach in the hall mirror. She heard Sean rustle in the bathroom. Through the floor-to-ceiling windows, the California sun set into a soft pink.

"Zip me up?" she asked when he appeared behind her. She felt Sean's hand on her hip as he gripped the zipper and pulled. She thought briefly that she should suck in her stomach and wondered if he gauged the bulk of her flesh with his hand, but brushed those thoughts away. Instead, she kept her head lowered and her hair pulled over her shoulder.

"There," he said. He gave the collar a gentle tug. "You look amazing."

"Thanks," she said. It was hard to accept a compliment, to fight the urge to protest, but it was something she'd worked on for the past four weeks.

"Shall we?" he asked. She took his arm as he led her to the elevator.

When they arrived, ushered through the sleek minimalistic restaurant by a woman in a tight black outfit, everyone was already gathered at the table. "Harper," Helena said, and rose with the elegance only a lifetime in the industry could ingrain into a person. "You look absolutely ravishing." She kissed her on either cheek, and Harper nearly teared up at the miasma of familiar European perfume that clung close to Helena. It brought back good memories of time in the house, of racing to go-sees with Molly in her early days, and of strong black coffee before dawn at the little chipped table while Helena poured advice on her.

As Helena released her, Joon-ki slapped Sean on the back and approached her. "I've heard a lot about you," he said. Harper raised her brows. "All good, of course," he said.

"And I've heard so much about you," Harper said. Joon-ki reached out a hand, but Harper pulled him close. He resisted for a moment, but quickly melted into her embrace. "Thank you," she whispered into his ear. "For taking care of him, for everything."

"It's my pleasure," he said.

"And who is *this*?" P asked as he snaked an arm around Harper's waist and drank in Joon-ki's slender figure. "I'm Philip, one 'p,'" he told Joon-ki. "Although, I personally think two p's are a lot more fun."

"P," Harper hissed at him. "Tone it down a little."

Joon-ki gave him a polite smile and went back to Sean.

"Not gay?" P mouthed at her. She shook her head and he sighed. "Damn. Well, I took a shot."

"Is that my dress?" Molly's husky voice asked from behind her.

"Molly!" she said. "Actually, believe it or not, it's mine. One of my few couture items that I didn't accidentally on purpose forget to give back."

"I'm not sure I believe you," Molly said with a playful lilt. "But either way, it looks better on you than it ever would on me. As per usual."

For the first time, Harper was aware of the cloying self-deprecation Molly gave off. *And it's not just her*, Harper thought. *It's all of us, every model that's been told we're too fat, too thick, too ethnic, or too anything else.* How had she not seen it for all these years? Sophia was right, the industry was in desperate need of a buoy, or preferably a life raft, for all these girls. Undoing the damage that they took daily required a first step. *Maybe I really can be that step after all*, she thought.

Molly was skirted on either side by more of Harper's old roommates. One had the telltale busted blood vessels in her eyes of a recent purging session. The other had curated a maxi dress with careful cutouts to highlight what Harper was sure she considered hard work. Her ribs were highlighted in the accent lighting and although she was twenty-two at the oldest, her knees already crinkled at the crest from a complete lack of fat and muscle in the legs.

"Hey," a low voice said from behind her. Harper felt a hand on her shoulder. "Good to know someone in the family loves sushi as much as I do."

Harper spun around. "Connor! What are you doing here?" she asked. "Where's Sam?" She craned her neck around the restaurant but didn't see her.

"Just flew in for the party!" he said. "And I'm solo for now. Thus the same-day flight back. Sam's going to have the baby any minute, but I didn't want to miss out on the festivities. It'll probably be the last adults-only soiree I can make in quite awhile. Sam sends her wishes. She'd loved to have come. I think not being able to indulge in sashimi would have done her in, though," he said with a wink.

"Well, I'm glad you made it," she said. "Are you going to get a chance to check out the property Sean found? It's incredible, really."

"I'm heading over after this," he said. "Although I saw the virtual tour and the photos, so I already know it's a fantastic find. Perfect for the company. And I'm excited you'll be working from there, too. It's good to have everyone in the same place. Sam's following in your footsteps after her maternity leave."

"Oh?"

"Yeah, she wants to open her own events management company on the West Coast. With supplies in a storage facility, she doesn't need that much overhead. At least not yet. But if she expands and brings on a lot of employees, who knows?"

"That's great!" she said. Having Sam at the same building helped ease Harper's nerves about her new position. Although she hadn't asked, Sam had the look of someone who'd at least dabbled with modeling in the past. She might be a good sounding board as Harper got started. More importantly, she knew she'd be a good friend.

"I'd like to thank everyone for coming," Sean said. The little group hushed as everyone found their seats. The waitstaff had snuck in between them to fill up small pots of warm sake. Seaweed salad rested on the small plates.

Harper smiled at Sean and he pulled her to his side. "Some of you know why I chose today for this little get-together." She stiffened. *Was he about to tell everybody that she was one month out of rehab?* Harper knew she'd eventually tell everyone. It would be pivotal in her own narrative of how she came to be an eating disorder community educator, but she wasn't sure if she was ready for that yet.

"Actually, a lot of events pointed to this date," Sean said. "And I won't bore you with all the details. I would like to say that on this date last year, I ... well, I wasn't anywhere close to being the person I am now. I was a mess. A lot of you know that, and if you didn't, well, now you do."

Harper squeezed his hand, grateful she wouldn't have to field awkward questions right away.

"I was having a particularly rough day. Or night, I should say. And—not even Harper knows this story—but I was walking home. It was almost sunrise, and I'd been out all night. I couldn't find my car and I was stubborn as hell—"

"Was?" Connor asked, but gave Sean a smile.

"Okay, still am," Sean conceded. "But I was hellbent on walking home, all twelve miles of it, from some bar or club on the other side of town. And I passed some little shrine set up near a Catholic church. It was temporary, I don't know if it was for a special event or what. But it was a Celtic display, and it just looked so out of place. So beautiful. I stopped, which was rare back then. I pretty much had tunnel vision for anything that was pure self-destruction. And there she was. Two of them, actually. Figures of these two girls with fire-red hair. In the most beautiful handwriting, there was the description of red-haired women considered sacred to the goddesses of war. That image, it always stayed with me. I believe it was the first time I even thought about fighting back against all the demons inside me. I just ... I didn't know she was real. Not until I met Harper."

"Aw!" Molly said, her puppy eyes huge with love.

"And today?" Sean said. "In front of all of you, the people we care about the most, I'd like to propose a toast." Sean lifted up his water glass that clinked with ice and handed Harper the small tumbler of sake. "Together, we've overcome a lot," he said, and he turned to her. "More than I imagine other couples manage in their first few months together. But it's been through the strength of our mutual love, support and sometimes flat out dogged determination that we made it through."

"Cheers," Harper said. The sounds of glasses kissing filled the air.

As Harper let the sweet, thick liquid make its way down her throat, Sean took her glass and set it on the table. "Harper, I couldn't have made it here without you," he said. "That's why ..."

Sean pulled a black box out of his jacket pocket as he dropped to one knee. Harper was briefly aware of the excited murmurs at the table, but soon everything except Sean faded away as her heart began to soar.

"Will you marry me?"

"Yes!" she said. Warm tears of joy pricked at her eyes. "Oh my god," she said. "I didn't know—"

Sean opened the box to reveal a large princess-cut diamond nestled in a halo band. He slid the ring onto her finger, a rose gold that complemented the dainty collar that hugged her neck. As he rose to his feet and pulled her to his chest, she felt a wholeness she didn't even know she'd missed. She was full, complete. And with him she knew, beyond any doubts, that she would always be happy.

ABOUT VIVIAN WOOD

Vivian likes to write about troubled, deeply flawed alpha males and the fiery, kick-ass women who bring them to their knees.

Vivian's lasting motto in romance is a quote from a favorite song: "Soulmates never die."

Be sure to follow Vivian through her Vivian's Vixens mailing list or Facebook group to keep up with all the awesome giveaways, author videos, ARC opportunities, and more!

VIVIAN'S WORKS
ADDICTION
OBSESSION

WILD HEARTS (COMING IN NOVEMBER)

DR. HOTTIE (COMING IN DECEMBER)

HIS VIRGIN
HIS BEST FRIEND'S LITTLE SISTER
CLAIMING HER INNOCENCE
HIS TO KEEP

PROMISE ME

Knocking Boots

SEAL's Bride
SEAL's Kiss
SEAL's Touch
Small Town Seals

Hard Up
Covet
Rock Me
Protection
Bad Boy Prince
Punt

For more information....
vivian-wood.com
info@vivian-wood.com

CPSIA information can be obtained
at www.ICGtesting.com
Printed in the USA
LVOW13s2043290118
564435LV00013B/1680/P